Spiral

L.A. Storm 4

RJ Scott

V.L. Locey

Love Lane Books

Copyright

Spiral (L.A. Storm, 4)

Copyright © 2024 RJ Scott, Copyright © 2024 V.L. Locey

Cover design by Meredith Russell, Edited by Sue Laybourn

Published by Love Lane Books Limited

ISBN - 9781785644917

All Rights Reserved

Spiral

When the worlds of academia and sports collide, a doctor of math and a dyslexic hockey star find that love has its own perfect equation.

Craig learned to skate as soon as he could walk, moving from figure skating to excelling in hockey and succeeding in both despite the challenges of his dyslexia. Visual aids, practical, hands-on learning, and the support of friends not only helped him in school but also honed his skills on the ice, making him a versatile and intuitive player. When he meets Jamie at a team party, Craig is instantly captivated by the handsome professor. Despite the lasting effects of a former abusive relationship that's still haunting him, they end up in bed. Craig's insecurities drive him away—after all, what can a professor possibly see in someone like him? His past relationship makes trusting Jamie hard. Thankfully, Jamie is not only persistent but also understanding, and despite his worries, Craig can't help but say yes. Falling for Jamie is as easy as slipping on fresh ice.

After his ex from hell stole his research and made him the academic community's laughingstock, Dr. Jameson "Jamie" Hennessy decided to reset his life and moved across the country to live with his best friend. With everything he worked so hard for now gone, Jamie needs funding to stay on the West Coast, and for that, he needs a new approach to his research. After one too many drinks at a team party, things heat up with a sexy hockey player he can't take his eyes off, but after the most incredible sex of his life, Craig leaves him alone in a cold bed the morning after. When Jamie's admiration for Craig and his obsession with mathematics collide, a new hypothesis about movement in sports is born. Could Craig be the answer he wasn't even looking for?

Dedication

To my family who accepts me and all my foibles and quirks. Even the plastic banana in my holster.
VL Locey

Always for my family.
RJ Scott

L.A. STORM #4

SPIRAL

RJ SCOTT & V.L. LOCEY

Love Lane Books

Chapter One

Jamie

I CAREFULLY PLACED THE LAST MINI SANDWICHES ONTO the colorful platter, stepping back to admire the spread of finger food that Scarlett, Daisy, and I had managed to whip up. The table was an artful mess of snacks created by me. I'd channeled my British father and my mom, former Miss Maine, who'd taken to living near London and being a Brit with extreme enthusiasm. They'd given me a mathematical brain, dual passports, an English accent, and a love of afternoon tea. I'd made tiny sandwiches, crudités, dips, small cakes, and, of course, scones and all the extras—ready for the afternoon crowd of ravenous hockey players and their families.

"Looks like we could feed an army, huh?" I chuckled, glancing down at Scarlett, who meticulously rearranged the carrot sticks.

She beamed up at me, her blue eyes sparkling with pride. "Dad's going to eat at least half of these," she declared confidently, her gaze sliding over to the sandwiches.

With her light blonde hair bouncing as she nodded vigorously, Daisy added, "And Jackson likes the sandwiches best. He told me last time!" Her tiny finger pointed toward the pile of sandwiches adorned with various toppings.

I smiled at their excitement. "Well, then, I think we've done a stellar job. High five, team!" I raised my hand, and they both smacked it with giggles.

Loud clattering on the stairs announced Oliver and Jackson's arrival from upstairs. I turned to see them descending the staircase, ready with a joke about a herd of elephants, Oliver's hand briefly clasping Jackson's. The two men, hopelessly in love, shared a quick, tender kiss at the bottom—a simple moment of affection that sent an unexpected twinge of envy through my chest.

I turned back to the table, arranging the LA Storm napkins to distract myself—I'd spent two hours sourcing the perfect purple for the table and the balloons. It's not that I expected people to notice this, but as my dad said, if something is worth doing, then it's worth doing right. I'd chosen an afternoon tea motif. I'd even hung bunting over the counters, and there were sandwiches, proper crisps I'd found in a trendy shop in Santa Monica, plus scones with pots of jam and cream. Or jelly, as Oli liked to call it, which is weird given that jelly is what I used to have as a kid. Back in the UK, our jelly was wobbly and sweet, unlike what Americans called jam. There was also a barbecue, but that was for later. First, the heathens making up the LA Storm would be introduced to the more sophisticated side of British cuisine—the perfect scone.

"Looks good, guys," Oliver said and clapped my shoulder.

I sent him my trademark smile, the one that said I wasn't jealous at all. It wasn't as if I *wanted Oliver*. He was my best friend, and I was genuinely happy for him, but we were always going to be just that—friends. Only witnessing that moment between him and Jackson highlighted the space beside me—a space I hadn't realized I was yearning to fill until Jackson had moved in and the four of us, Oliver, Scarlett, Daisy, and me, had become five. I couldn't even hate Jackson. He was a hot mess, all intense and scowling at times, but Oli loved him, and his love was smoothing all of Jackson's rough edges. I liked Jackson. I like Jackson for Oli.

But I missed holding hands, kissing, or sharing a coffee and crossword with someone.

I thought I'd had that with Sean.

Arsehole-wanker-Sean, fellow mathematics genius and my former boyfriend, who proved everyone right by not only ruining my entire bloody life but, more importantly, stealing my research and undermining my credibility.

Jackson caught my eye and smiled as they approached. "London! This spread looks fantastic!"

That was a new thing Jackson had started doing, calling me London. He gave everyone nicknames, and he'd chosen mine because of being a Brit, of drinking tea, and calling everyone a wanker.

He's the wanker.

Still, part of me liked the moniker, even if I sent him my best haughty Lord-of-the-manor snarl every time he used it—not that my reaction had any effect.

He wrinkled his nose at me but carried on talking. "The girls have been bragging about their chef skills all morning," he said.

Oliver ruffled Scarlett's hair, surveying the table. "Looks like you've outdone yourselves again. Thanks, Jamie."

I shrugged, a half-smile playing on my lips. "It's nothing. It keeps me busy, and I enjoy it." Glancing over at Jackson, who was already reaching for a sandwich, I teased, "Make sure you save some for the others, Columbo."

Jackson blinked at me, "Columbo? Really?"

I tilted my chin. "It was the most derogatory nickname I could think of," I announced.

Jackson bit his lip, probably trying to hold back a laugh. "I love it," he said and knuckled my arm, which, ouch, he didn't know his strength. Then he laughed and popped the sandwich into his mouth. "And no promises on the food, London," he mumbled through a mouthful, earning him an eye roll from Oliver and giggles from the girls.

The doorbell chimed, signaling the arrival of the first guests. Daisy sprinted to the door, Scarlett on her heels, their laughter trailing behind them as they raced to open it.

I gave the snack arrangement one last tweak as Oli and Jackson headed to the door. Would people hate my idea? They were here for a barbecue, and me making all of this was probably going to end up being the butt of jokes. For a moment, I panicked and thought about swiping the whole lot into the trash. The colorful food seemed small, overshadowed by the buzzing energy filling the house as big hockey players arrived, partners in tow, kids shouting, laughing. I felt a familiar pang of nerves. I liked people in general, but I wasn't good with chaos. People streamed in, shedding jackets and greeting each other with enthusiastic handshakes and warm hugs. The room was loud, with a mixture of laughter and conversations, plus the faint sounds of a hockey game on the TV in the background. *It didn't take long for hockey to be front and center.*

Oliver was already amid it all, clasping hands and giving hearty handshakes. "Hey, Ash!" he called out, drawing my attention to his defensive partner, who entered with a grin. They did the whole bro-hug thing, and then Ash hurried over to me, and we exchanged the customary fist bump, his grin contagious.

"I need one of those biscuit things," he announced. "Oli said you have them with jelly and heavy cream, right?"

I laughed, both at his eagerness and his description. "You mean scones, Ash. They're scones, not biscuits. And yes, we've got them—complete with jam and clotted cream, not jelly and heavy cream. It's a British delicacy, not a rodeo snack." I was lying—it wasn't a delicacy, but it *was* bloody delicious.

Ash raised his eyebrows, clearly amused. "Man, you Brits have a weird way of naming your food. But if it tastes as good as it looks, you can call it whatever you want."

He wandered off toward the food table. I shook my head, chuckling as Oliver approached me and clapped me on the shoulder.

"Your scones are a hit, Jamie. Even if half the team can't say 'clotted cream' without making a face."

"It's the simple joys of educating Americans on the finer points of English cuisine," I deadpanned, the snark in my voice tinged with affection. "Someone has to elevate your culinary experiences. Can't have you living off hot dogs and popcorn forever."

Our banter was cut short as more guests arrived, each greeted by Oliver's booming voice and warm handshakes.

And there he was.

Craig.

I hadn't been watching for him at all.

Nope.

He was here, a five-foot-ten-inch cute but lethal hockey player. Fast and deadly, he was feared by defensemen all over the NHL for his crafty, squirrely speed. He was dressed in slim-fit cutoffs and a T-shirt that clung to every one of his sexy lines. He arrived alone—I think—with no sign of a girlfriend or boyfriend, and he moved through the crowd with smiles and happiness. He was already halfway through his first beer, with another in his other hand.

As his eyes met mine, the noise of the party faded into a distant murmur. I was so drawn to him, even though he was everything the men I'd previously dated were not: shorter than me, wiry, an air of easy confidence despite the chaos of fame hockey had thrust upon him. His relaxed demeanor here was a stark contrast to his on-ice reputation.

Despite how idiotic it would be to get physical with one of Oli's teammates, I wanted him.

As our gazes locked, I felt something like hope that maybe he'd come over for a scone and I could dazzle him with something witty. I straightened my favorite dark blue waistcoat. I wore them as a kind of armor, a way of breaking the ice, playing into being a Brit, having something quirky and just for me, but his gaze dropped to my fingers adjusting the fit, and when he glanced up at me, something inexplicable shadowed his expression. It wasn't discomfort, but there was a retreat, a subtle drawing back that seemed at odds with the smile he offered everyone else. He turned away, weaving through the crowd, a trail of light laughter marking his path. He was utterly unreachable, and I couldn't help but wonder what I'd done.

Because it had to be me.

My social skills were either at the level of Scarlett and Daisy—I knew all the words to every Disney movie—or at the level of fellow academics. Every other situation was fraught with danger.

We'd spoken only once before, an encounter that had started promisingly enough. He'd teased me about my accent, and in response, I had exaggerated my Britishness, rolling out my best King's English, which had drawn a laugh from him and a playful declaration that I was cute. Flustered, I'd returned the compliment, called him cute, and for a second, he'd frowned, then it had cleared, and he blushed. Maybe it was being called cute? He wasn't as big as some of the other players, so was it that I implied he was small? I recall getting flustered, but the conversation had quickly spiraled into academia—with what I thought was a light, flirty discussion about Fibonacci sequences. He'd seemed interested until suddenly, he wasn't. His words had tangled, and he'd excused himself abruptly, leaving me bewildered and concerned I'd crossed a line I hadn't seen.

Now, watching him at the party, the ease with which he interacted with others made our previous encounter all the more confusing. Did he think I wasn't cute after all? The thought nagged at me, a persistent whisper amidst the clinks of glasses and bursts of laughter.

I tried to shake off the feeling, focusing on the guests instead, explaining that jam went on the scone first and, no, clotted cream wasn't a dipping sauce and needed to be spread, but my gaze was drawn repeatedly to Craig as he moved through the room. He was in the corner with Scarlett and a couple of the wives, touching his toes, everyone laughing as they copied him. He was so... bendy... and when he went into the splits, I nearly choked on a slice of cucumber.

The things I could do to a man that flexible...

Why he seemed to avoid me now, after what had felt like a connection, was a puzzle, but after the first shot of whiskey, my edges smoothed, and with the second, I felt as if I could talk to him. After the third and fourth, with him downing beer like water, I felt as if I could take on the world.

He excused himself and headed upstairs to the bathroom, laughing and joking, taking the stairs two at a time, and, bloody hell, I was after him like a dog on a bone. I found him at the top of the stairs, nowhere near the bathroom, but instead tucked into a small reading nook the kids used, his head in one hand, a beer loose in the other.

He was slumped and exhausted, and he hadn't heard me there.

"Craig?" I asked.

He lifted his gaze slowly, all kinds of resigned. "Jamie," he said in reply.

I had a hundred things I wanted to ask him or tell him, but a whiskey brain is different from a normal brain, and I yelled the first thing I could think of.

"Why do you hate me?"

Chapter Two

Craig

HATE HIM? WHAT THE ACTUAL HELL WAS HE EVEN TALKING about?

My attraction to Jamie Hennessy was about as far from hate, as I was from winning a national speed-reading contest.

Dropping my hand from my muzzy head, I stared at him for what must have seemed like eons to the poor guy. The beer bottle in my hand felt heavier than it should, given it was two swigs from being empty.

"Do you plan to answer? Or are you just going to stare at me as if I have a marching band on top of my bloody head?" he demanded. Then, because he was so fucking adorable, he reached up to feel the top of his head as if he thought there might actually *be* a marching band residing on that perfectly combed chestnut hair of his. No matter the occasion, he was always wearing fashionable clothes, vests, ties, slacks, or casual flair, with his scruff just so, his hair gelled to perfection, which was the complete word for Jamie. Perfection. From his clothes to his accent to his sexy-as-sin glasses framing stunning blue eyes. The man was flawless.

"Hate isn't..." My throat was suddenly dry. I gulped the dregs of my beer. I'd had a few too many, but I wasn't driving because I'd been in a shit place after getting a call from my asshole ex-boyfriend and knew I'd be drowning my sorrows in water, yeast, hops, and malts. No person could make me feel like a dumb loser faster than Leon. "I don't hate you."

"No? We talked once, and now you won't even look at me." He listed to the left, and I reached out to steady him, dropping my empty drink onto the floor, which rolled away. He shrugged me off. "Don't touch me unless you plan to take me into my room and ravage my arse." He pressed his hands to his mouth as if those words were never meant to see the light of day. "Sorry," he muttered, then tilted his chin. "No, not sorry, I meant that." Then, he ruined the air of confidence with a hiccup.

All the oxygen left the second floor of Oliver's huge house. The noise from the party vanished. The area around us seemed to shimmer with something that was either a cloud of purple lust—and why lust was purple, I don't know, unless it had something to do with Prince, who was the king of passion and desire—or I'd knocked back way too many Blue Moons.

"Okay. I'll ravage your arse," I said softly, reaching for him, my fingers curling around the back of his neck to pull his mouth to mine.

He blinked in surprise, and I thought he might step back, but he came without any resistance, his lips so soft and warm and tasting of a top-shelf rye whiskey. The burst of cloves, black pepper, and cinnamon rushed in as his lips parted to allow me access. Our tongues tangled. His hands were everywhere. I cradled his skull in my palms. The few inches of height he had over me only added to the explosion of desire now flaming out of control in my veins. I loved being able to snuggle into a taller man. Not that I was super short, but in hockey, anyone under six feet was a hobbit.

His hands settled on my ass. I tipped his head to the left. He gave my cheeks a hard squeeze, moaned into my mouth, and then he dragged me up another flight of stairs and opened a door. Somehow, I'd credit it to my innate grace and athletics—not—we managed to stay on our feet as we stumbled through it. The room was a bit of a blur: windows, curtains, a dresser, a desk, and a big bed. The bed looked inviting, neatly made with rich blue coverings and fancy decorative round pillows. The room smelled of his cologne, a heady, clean citrus scent that enticed me. A small light on the bedstand was lit, casting our shadows over the wall as we bumbled around, unwilling to let go of the other to walk.

"God, you taste good," I huffed over his puffy lips. The scratch of his stubble on my cheek as I tongued my way to his neck was gasoline to a fire already out of control. The door closed behind us with a click. My hands carded into his hair. My teeth worked at his throat, nipping sharply, each little bite making him groan in pleasure. "Like man and… uhm… fuck words."

"Right, fuck words. Who needs words?" he huffed as he pulled at my belt, the brush of the back of his fingers over my erection sending hot spikes of want to my cock.

"Words are for losers who use too many vocables to try to counter—"

"You're talking too much," I snarled, sucking a hot path from his collarbone to his ear. God, I hoped two flights up was enough to stop anyone from hearing us, and I placed a hand over his mouth. "Shhh, everyone could hear."

"No one can hear us up here," he protested as I tugged in his earlobe with my teeth, my fingers keeping his head tilted just right for maximum neck ravaging. "I just talk a lot when I'm nervous or excited."

"Which are you now?" I eased back, releasing his lobe to stare at him. His cheeks were rosy under those short whiskers, his pupils blown behind glasses askew on his perfect face. Seeing him all rumpled and knowing it had been my hands doing all the rumpling made my dick even harder. But, if he were nervous or not feeling what seemed to be us falling into the nearest bed to fuck each other silly, then I'd back off.

"I'm *incredibly excited*." He reached up to remove my hand from his hair and lead it to the bulge in his slacks. Fuck. He was rigid as a board. Was he cut or uncut? I couldn't wait to find out.

"Cool." I covered his mouth with mine.

He shuddered and sighed, then went back to getting me naked. My belt was ripped from the loops of my pants. I sucked on his tongue and then lapped deeply into his hot mouth. A wordy mouth. A mouth full of words that kept wanting to spill out of him like water from a fountain as he lowered my zipper. I rubbed the length of him with my palm. He began to melt into me, his knees buckling, and he went to his knees.

Feeling more than a little drunk and a lot worried about him passing out, I placed a finger under his chin. "Are you going to pass out?"

"Nope, I'm going to suck your cock."

Ah, well, that was fine then. He wet his lips. I nearly came right then and there. I threw a hand out to the nearest wall as he stripped me from the waist down in a blur.

"And what a lovely cock you have," he purred, taking my dick in hand and then gently rubbing his chin and cheek over the purplish head like a cat. The burn made me shiver, and my balls drew up.

"The things your mouth says," I panted as he tongued at my slit.

His yummy sounds as his tongue cleaned up my slick cock just about did me in. I thrust forward, fingers cupping his chin. He opened wide, his glasses now dangling from one ear. I plucked them from his face and dropped them to a dresser on my right as I fed him my cock. He took it all. Right to the root. My eyes rolled back. His mouth was capable of more than making words filled with intelligence and wit. His mouth could bring a grown man to his knees in seconds.

"Stop, I'm… fuck… too… close."

He pulled off, eyes now on me as my cockhead lingered on his lower lip. "I'm glad you let me know. I want you to come inside me."

"I… we should… I'm on PrEP and am negative and… Shit. Oh shit." He tongued the slit again, teasing a small droplet to appear that he then licked off. "I just... right, tested."

"Same." He rose, saliva glistening his chin and lips, and I captured his mouth again.

We kissed our way to the bed. A bed that I hoped was his. "Is this your room?"

"Yes. Mine." He then proceeded to strip off his clothes. His body was finely made and lithe, with some brown curls spattered over his chest, then thickening the farther down my eyes traveled. A thick uncut cock sprang free. I'd never been with an uncut man. I wanted to mouth his dick, taste and play with his foreskin, and get to know the feel of it between my lips. His hand wrapped around his prick. He eased the foreskin back and milked some pre-cum out. "Bed."

He stumbled over his discarded clothing, sniggered madly, and fell on top of me. I laughed at his arrival, then all the laughter faded as he wiggled around, his lips brushing mine, his cock rutting into my belly.

"Ride me," I grunted. "Ride me hard."

"So lazy," he replied as he settled on my thighs, his cock leaking over his fingers as he continued to stroke himself. "Making me do all the work."

"You can handle it," I countered.

He pinched my nipple as he smiled wickedly. "Oh yes, I'll handle it."

I watched, spellbound, as he yanked open a drawer on the nightstand with too much enthusiasm, sending the lamp to the carpet with a soft thud. "Bollocks, we'll worry over that later," he muttered as he fisted the lube.

I yearned to touch him all over but lay there, unable to

move at the sight of him flicking open the lid and squeezing out a lot of lube, reaching down and starting to prep himself. I was stunned, unable to move, and did nothing but watch his sexy freaking fingers in his sexy freaking hole.

"That's a lot of lube," he said, his fingers coated with slick, and he stared at it as if he couldn't recall what he was doing.

"Are you okay?" I asked, and he removed his slick fingers from his hole, took hold of the tube with both hands, and squeezed a glob the size of an Easter ham onto my chest. I gasped in shock. Jamie splayed over me, lube smooshing out between us as if we were overstuffed Oreos. The sound was atrocious but hot. As was the slip-slide of his body over mine. I grabbed at his head to lead his mouth to my lips. He slithered off to the left with a snort of amusement, righted himself on top of me, and then eased his tight hole down over my cock. I forgot all about kissing him. I arched up, trying to get a hold of his hips, but was unable to. He winced and moaned as I dug my heels into the mattress, my fingers biting into the edge of the bed. His ass was magical. Hot as hell, tight as a fist, and slick.

"Fucking hell. Your cock."

"Your hole is so tight," I managed to croak out.

Dirty talk wasn't my forte. When I had a gorgeous man riding my dick, my brain tended to short out. Thankfully, having sex didn't require me to read a manual. Jamie and I were doing just fine. Better than fine. As he began to undulate on my cock, I boosted the word from fine to extraordinary. I slapped my hands on his chest so I could pluck at his tight, dark nipples. He went from sexy, polished intellectual to unfettered wild man in the blink of an eye.

"Keep that... doing that... fucking hell yes!" he shouted, his lean thighs powering him up and down like the pistons on a steamship engine.

Wow, my head was still with the ships to some extent. Super. I pumped up into Jamie to drive the niggling boat info from my skull and was pleased to see he liked when I did that. He liked it a lot. His mouth formed a perfect *O*, and his head fell back. I did it again with more energy, and his bouncing cock spurted as he roared his release. I took him in hand, stroking his pulsing dick, eager to mix the scent of his cum into the cloud of cologne, sex, and whatever floral smell was on the sheets.

"Did I hit your sweet spot?" I asked roughly.

"Yes, yes, oh fucking fuck yes!"

"Good to know." I pounded up into him, each glide into his snug channel rushing me closer to my orgasm. When it hit, and it hit like a shoulder check from a rampaging buffalo, I howled like a wolf. Jamie rode me slowly, rolling his hips, milking me with his constricting ass until I had to beg him to stop.

"That was just... yeah... perfect," he huffed, then fell over me, his nose buried in my neck, his softening cock pinned between us in a thick coating of cum and lube. I flopped an arm over his back, balls still pumping spunk into his ass, and smiled at the ceiling.

"Yeah, so perfect," I mimicked in a dreadful British accent.

He snorted like a pig and then promptly fell sound

asleep. Not wanting to shift even if I could, I inhaled the scent of us as my eyes grew heavier and heavier. A short nap would be fantastic. Just a few minutes to catch our breaths, and then we'd do something about the cum gluing us together.

Yep, just a five-minute power nap, and everything would be all... sorted... out.

Chapter Three

Jamie

I WOKE WITH MY HEAD HAMMERING TO A SCREAMING alarm, and as I peeled my eyes open, the sunlight streaming through the blinds felt like an assault. Why hadn't I shut the blinds? Every movement was sluggish, each thought fighting through a fog.

"Fuck my life," I muttered; my mouth tasted like something had died in it. I made the age-old promise that I would never drink again. Ever. I couldn't recall what had happened, as I regretted all my life choices, and then it hit me, and the regrets changed from me over drinking to me throwing myself at a man who'd been avoiding me.

"Bollocks," I told the curtains.

Slowly, the room came into focus—the familiar mess of clothes strewn about, the bottle of water on the bedside table, my clock showing it was six-thirty a.m. And then, the emptiness of the bed next to me sank in as I shifted to face where Craig had been, a twinge in my arse underscoring the fact that, yep, there had been sex.

So, I hadn't imagined him... he had been here, hadn't he?

I sat up, my head protesting with a sharp jab of pain, and surveyed the room. No sign of the sexy skater. No note, no forgotten jacket. Nothing but the tangled sheets bearing the unmistakable, slick evidence of last night's escapades. The lube was everywhere—on the sheets, a testament to my drunken state and the speed with which lust had grabbed us. I grimaced at the mess, the physical residue making his absence more pronounced.

He'd gone.

Had it meant anything to him? The night had blurred into a sequence of sex, touches, and laughter. It had felt real, felt right. But the space beside me spoke of a different truth—one where he'd slipped away without a word, leaving me to wake alone with my thoughts and this throbbing headache.

Great. Just great.

I swung my legs out of bed, the cool air hitting my skin, making me shiver. I should clean up and start erasing the traces of what had happened before someone saw it. Yet, I hesitated, a part of me not ready to wipe away the last vestiges of his presence, messy though they were. What if last night was just the one time? What if he'd been avoiding me for a reason and then gotten drunk, and I'd gotten drunk, and then we'd made equally bad decisions?

As I sat there, the weight of those decisions pressed heavily upon me. What had I been thinking? Random sex wasn't me. I wasn't a man who went for reckless encounters, especially not with someone like Craig—

someone I liked and maybe wanted more than one night with.

"Bollocks," I repeated, this time louder, while digging my fingers in my hair and holding tight before letting go long enough to down the water, then stumbled, tired, into the bathroom. My ass ached, my back ached, and the muscles in my thighs burned, but the memory of the best orgasm I'd ever had flooded me, and when I faced the mirror, my hair sticking up all over, I was smiling.

Until I saw the marks on my neck.

Clearly, Craig had vampiric tendencies by the bruises he'd left. I wish I could remember every one of them being made, but no, I was the idiot who'd drunk too much and made questionable life choices. The shower helped a little. I mean, it didn't wash away the ache in my arse, or the ring of bruises at the base of my throat, or the handprint on my left thigh where he'd gripped me, but it cleared my head a little, and at least I wasn't sick.

But there it was, the stark, sticky reality of our choices smeared across my sheets. I sighed deeply, frustration and resignation settling in as I stripped the bed and rolled the sheets into a ball. I'd need to face him eventually, face whatever this was—or wasn't—between us. But not just yet. First, I needed tea. And headache pills. Lots of them.

When I shuffled downstairs, the kitchen was unexpectedly silent. There was no sign of the girls yet, but I was on breakfast duty because Oliver had an early practice. I'd braced myself for the typical whirlwind of activity stirred up by Scarlett and Daisy. Instead, I found immaculate counters and the remnants of yesterday's event gone.

With a sense of relief that I had silence for a while, my hands fumbled as I filled the kettle. The promise of tea and headache meds kept me anchored to the world this morning.

As the kettle began to rumble with the early signs of a boil, the sound was a gentle murmur compared to the throbbing in my head. I leaned against the counter, closing my eyes briefly, letting the familiar ritual of making tea soothe the rough edges of my hangover.

Oliver's booming entrance shattered the moment. "Morning, sunshine!" he declared with a grin far too bright for this ungodly hour.

The greeting hit me like a sledgehammer. I winced, opening one eye to squint at my best friend, who would die quickly if he didn't rein it in. "You're too loud," I muttered, my voice hoarse.

Oliver was already dressed in his Storm T-shirt, the epitome of morning readiness that I found particularly offensive given my current state. "Sorry," he chuckled, his voice dropping to what he probably thought was a whisper but was still average speaking volume.

"Tablets," I whimpered and focused on finding the right tea bag while he unlocked the medicine box. I accepted the bottle of painkillers he slid across the counter to me with extreme gratitude. I popped a couple, chased them down with a swig of water, made my mug of tea, and then buried my head in my hands with my elbows propped awkwardly on the counter.

Oliver's presence was a mix of comfort and annoyance —a brother in all but blood who knew exactly when to push and when to hold back. As I sat there, my head cradled in my hands, I felt him pat my back sympathetically.

"Rough night?" he asked, his tone laced with a brotherly concern that I both appreciated and dreaded.

I nodded into my hands, not quite ready to dive into the details of last night's escapades or Craig's silent departure. "You could say that," I mumbled, my voice muffled by my palms.

"You don't normally drink," he said after a pause, pulling out a tray of eggs, six of which I knew would disappear into whatever omelets he would make. It was all about protein for Mr. Hockey Star, but the thought of eggs right now for me... gah, no. "Is it the ex from hell? Did he do something else?"

"Sean? Haven't heard anything since he handed over our research with my name removed," I grumbled, but I wasn't going to go through all that again, particularly with a headache. "I just..." What did I say? That I thought Craig was ignoring me, so I got drunk, and then I pouted and went all psycho on him, and then he ran away? I sighed, a part of me relieved to have a friend like Oli to confide in, another part wishing I could rewind and start yesterday over so I had nothing to explain. But for now, tea sounded like a perfect first step, and I sipped the brew, the heat of which soothed my throat. I remembered a messy three a.m. blowjob.

Or did I dream rolling over and swallowing him down, near choking on his glorious cock and—

"Earth to Jamie, come in, Jamie," Oli said as he waved his hand in front of my face.

"It's all good," I lied.

He patted my shoulder as if he understood I needed to lie, before plating up his enormous omelet and finishing it just as Jackson strolled into the kitchen in his cop suit, not looking quite as ragged as he used to before he'd moved in here with Oli and started eating correctly and actually having a supply of new ties at his beck and call. He and Oli exchanged a kiss, and then he swung his leg over the stool and rested his head on his hands, staring at me.

"So, I caught someone breaking out," he deadpanned, and for a moment I tensed. Someone had broken into our house. Were the girls okay? Surely Oli would be upset if…

Wait…

Someone had broken *out* of the house.

He waited for me to put two and two together before grinning at me.

Arsehole wanker bastard.

He smirked, and when I glanced at Oli, I saw him biting his lip to stop an unmistakable grin. "Fuck you both backward," I snarled, and then after a few more sips of tea, I sighed. "Yes, it was Craig, and yes, we slept together, and yes, we were both drunk, and no, I don't want to talk about it."

"At least your walk of shame was only down the stairs; I had to help your spurned lover with the alarm and the gate and ensure he got in the cab." Jackson was teasing, but I was worried about Craig and what we'd done, and I didn't feel like joking.

"I didn't spurn him. Who even uses the word spurn."

Jackson shrugged. "Brits."

I scowled at him. "We don't say that."

"I've watched *Downton Abbey and Bridgerton*."

Jackson was baiting me into the usual US versus UK language thing, but I was done with his teasing. Why was it that anyone I met here expected me to talk like some straitlaced, uptight historical figure?

I changed the subject quickly. "Was he okay?" *Was he ashamed? Did he have regrets? Was he running?*

"Seemed okay to me," Jackson said.

"Really?"

"Really. He said he had an early practice, moaned about how it was the day after our event and how he shouldn't have drunk and..." He tapped the counter as he recalled more. "Oh yeah, he had a message for you."

Fuck, why didn't Jackson start with that? "What did he say?" Jackson was focused on pouring coffee into a thermos, then he kissed Oli, and I swear that man was out to make me hit him square on the nose.

"He said to tell you goodbye."

"That was it?" I was disappointed; part of me hoped Craig's words would be meaningful.

"Well..." He leaned toward me and lowered his voice as if he had another part of the message for my ears only; I moved in eagerly. "Yep, that was it," he said, stole one last kiss from Oli, grabbed his keys, and vanished.

"I hate him," I muttered.

Oli chuckled. "No, you don't."

"Yes. I do." I collapsed back to the counter, scrubbing at my eyes.

As I nursed my second hot mug of tea, feeling the life seep back into me, Oliver rested against the countertop, his gaze thoughtful.

"Craig's really something on the ice. Fast, smart. It's

like he's playing chess out there," he started, breaking the comfortable silence between us as I sipped my tea. "But he's also one of the nicest guys I've ever met. Always has time for everyone, always there to help the rookies."

I nodded, my grip on the mug tightening just a bit. I was warm inside as Oli said this.

"I messed it up."

"How?"

"I don't remember, but I know this is all my fault."

"If you don't remember, how do you know it's all your fault?"

"I'm British; it's always our fault," I murmured, and Oli chuckled again. "Also, he's not here, is he!" I waved at the kitchen. "I don't remember what I did, but he's the one running before I woke up."

"Craig is one of the good guys, and he would have needed to sleep before practice. I bet he didn't really want to go, so don't let one awkward morning make you think otherwise."

His words were meant to be reassuring, and somewhere beneath the headache, they were. But they also reminded me of a) why I was never drinking again and b) how awkward the morning after the night before could be.

Before I could respond, Oliver glanced at the clock and cursed softly. "I've got to head out. Practice won't wait for the weary or the hungover," he said with a grin, clapping me on the shoulder as he passed by on his way to the door. "Take care of the munchkins, yeah?"

"I'll do that," I replied, the reality of the day ahead settling on my shoulders as he disappeared out the door, the sound of it closing echoing slightly in the quiet kitchen. I was in charge of breakfast and getting the girls ready for school, and then it was head down, working out my next research project. Now, if my head survived this hangover, I had to start again.

Dr Jameson Hennessy, time of brain cell death, oh-seven-fifteen.

The sound of feet thumping down the stairs broke the peace. Scarlett and Daisy burst into the kitchen, their faces bright with the boundless energy of youth I envied on mornings like these.

"Jamie! We decided on teddy bear pancakes!" Daisy declared in a high-pitched demand that brooked no argument.

Scarlett nodded vigorously. "With lots of syrup! And strawberries!"

I set my mug down with a resigned smile, the remnants of my earlier contemplations about Craig fading as the immediate needs of Oliver's daughters took precedence. "All right, teddy bear pancakes it is," I said, pushing aside the nausea and the whole spinning head thing, pulling out the ingredients and firing up the grill.

As I mixed the batter and poured it into the shapes they demanded, the breakfast chaos took over, leaving no room for lingering thoughts of why Craig had gone without a goodbye, how embarrassing I'd been, or what might have been had he stayed. The kitchen filled with the scent of pancakes and the sound of delighted laughter, pulling me firmly back into the present. Here, now, this was what mattered. The rest would have to wait.

Chapter Four

Craig

As far as days went, this one was starting poorly.

No. Poorly wasn't a strong enough word. Poorly seemed too mild. Shitful. Yes, that was better. Today had started and was progressing shitfully. Perhaps that wasn't grammatically correct terminology, and sue me if it wasn't, but this morning was a heaping pile of dung.

I'd come awake around four in the morning after some of the best sex I'd ever experienced, with a triple dose of a killer beer headache, a cottonmouth, and my backside glued to some incredibly sticky sheets. Jamie, looking truly gorgeous in repose, stretched out beside me and made a smile appear for a second. And then reality stormed in and destroyed me with its big realness hammer. I'd scrambled out of the bed and shot to my feet. I'd been naked, covered with cum and lube, and experiencing a flashback that nearly toppled me into a panic attack.

"Stupid," I whispered as I slithered down in my seat in

the video room to watch game tapes with the rest of the team. I'd weaseled my way out of morning skate by saying I had diarrhea. Coach seemed dubious, Oli looked even more unconvinced, and Cameron tried to get me to drink some holistic green sludge his neighbor had recommended, which he now swore by. I'd passed on the olive-colored colon cleanser. If I had the runs, would I want something to make me run more? No, I would not.

The room was empty, save for me. The lights were low, the AC was cranking away, and my head was full of doubts, worries, and fears. I'd done the stupid thing again. The one thing I had vowed never to do again. I'd allowed myself to become obsessed with a beautiful, intelligent, man then because my dick ruled the fucking roost after a six-pack of beer; I'd then slept with said smart, sexy man.

"Stupid," I mumbled angrily to the empty room once more. This was exactly how things had started with Leon. I'd been drawn to him just as I was to Jamie. His smarts were a turn-on, no doubt, and something I admired greatly. Brainy guys were hot.

No. No. Brainy guys are mean, cruel, sadistic jerks.

Right. Yes, intelligent men were jerks. They came on to you, used all those fancy words and their nerdy good looks to seduce you, and then once they had you, they began chipping away at your self-confidence. They took you to intellectual events, then made snide comments during the damn colloquium about how they would have to explain the points and counterpoints to you later. They showed you off in public, fawned over you in front of the world, and then took you home and criticized you for being too dimwitted to reply to one of their colleagues in a manner befitting the boyfriend of *the* Schmied of Schmied, Tolliver, and Lawrence.

"Stupid," I whispered as the memories of my two years with Leon rolled over me like a boulder, flattening the self-esteem I'd worked so hard to rebuild after finally ending it with him. A year after I left his abusive ass, here I was, right back in the thick of things with another brainy man who would, over time, start to pick at my faults. Yes, I was dyslexic, but that didn't mean I was stupid. I'd fucking graduated college. Harvard, thank you very much. I had a degree just like Leon and Jamie—well, maybe not *exactly like* them. Leon was an attorney, and Jamie was a scientist. I'd gotten a degree in special education. Yes, it had been tough having to get special assistance and aids like text in audio, help with note-taking, and getting extended time on papers and exams. That didn't make me lesser, though. I had studied my heart out while playing college hockey. I knew for a fact that Leon had never balanced academics with athletics, so fuck all the way off.

I huffed out an exasperated sigh that made my head twinge. Fucking hell. I'd been doing so well. Well? Doing well? What. Ever. *Fuck.* And I really liked Jamie. He was cute, funny, and had that adorable accent. He was good with kids, too, which was a significant plus for me as I hoped to someday have a couple of my own and teach kids with learning disabilities. Mom and Dad were always harping about having a career lined up after hockey. Well, I did, and it might not make me lots of money or win me any fancy scientific awards, but seeing the light of understanding in a student's eyes would be its own reward. Of course, paying teachers well would be incredibly nice.

We, as a country, needed to prioritize these wages since teachers were the ones who educated the next generation.

The lights flickered on. I blinked and moaned. Oli strolled in with Cam and Charlie Zhang, the captain of the Storm and one of the nicest guys ever.

"You look rough," Cam offered, dropping down to my right while Charlie took the seat on the other side of Cameron. Oli sat to my left, his gaze touching on me briefly before he shifted his attention to the clock on the wall. Odd and suspicious. "Seriously, I can get Finn to run some of his avocado/kiwi/prune mixes over. He's home for a few weeks between shoots. I know we have some in the fridge. Rottie has been on this colon cleansing thing of late and—"

"No, thanks, I don't need to loosen my bowels," I insisted, sliding down even farther in my seat as the rest of the team filed in, most with wet heads from recent showers. A few shot me looks of commiseration. I smiled meekly at the kindness, then tugged my purple Storm cap to my eyebrows.

The room was loud now; the steady chatter of twenty-five men added to the thrum inside my head. Oliver and Charlie were talking about last night's party. Cam was on his phone, thumbs flying, probably having a lovey-dovey talk with his famous actor boyfriend. I also pulled out my phone and opened a book I was currently listening to. I loved fantasy and had found a complete audio set of *The Lord of the Rings* on sale, so I grabbed it up. There was no way this could work for me as printed word, but I would enjoy the audio. As I dug out my Bluetooth earbuds from the front pocket of my jeans, a text rolled in with a buzz.

Fearing it might be Claudia, my sister, who had this sixth sense when I did something stupid, I chanced a peek at the name as it flashed on the screen.

Leon.

My tender stomach roiled. Fuck. Think of the devil and up he pops, as my father liked to say. If only Dad knew how vile of a person Leon Schmied was, he might not be so confused as to why I'd left him in the middle of the night last summer. My throat felt tight. I swallowed several times to stem the wave of anxiety and nausea seeing his name brought. I should have been expecting the text. He sent two a week. He always asked me to return to him, saying he was sorry he'd been unwittingly unkind. Unwittingly, my ass. He reveled in shoving his big brain into the face of anyone who didn't have an IQ of a hundred and sixty-five. We got it. He was gifted. Those of us who were average should have gotten credit for getting a high school diploma. For the love of—

"Let's put the phones away and pay attention," Coach announced as he strode into the video room, coffee in hand, wearing a Storm hoodie and a look of consternation. "The Rebels are in our house tomorrow night. We owe them a beating for sending us packing in the finals. I never forget. I'm like a fucking pachyderm. So, we'll spend the next hour trying to figure out how to break their power play and… glad you could join us, Phillipe."

Our goalie slipped in like a tomcat returning home after roaming the neighborhood for a week.

"Sorry, Coach, I am not recouped from the shindig last night," Phillipe answered, then sat to Oliver's left, his big brown gaze skimming over the small group of out and proud queer players, of which he was one. "Cam'ron is not sick, Oliver is not sick, and Charles is also not sick. But I am with Craig and much sick. I think it makes us who are the most sensitive in the brain sickest when we douse our mental matters with alcohol, oui?"

"Yes, sure," I said, then got a gentle nod from the big French-Canadian goalie.

The team knew about my dyslexia. Sometimes, I had to have longer to grasp the plays on the white boards when they were sketched out. Then I would have to walk or skate the play. It took me far longer to get through the thick playbooks we had, but everyone was incredibly cool about giving me aid when I requested it. Not that I asked often. I'd been the same as a kid when I competed in pairs figure skating with Claudia. Our coach handled me differently than my sister, and it worked out. I had most of the plays committed to memory, but when the coaches brought in something new or changed a set pattern, I needed more time to get it down. Things were much more accessible now than when I'd been younger and had been trying to drink in all the *X*'s and *O*'s with a brain that liked to spin letters in circles.

Happy for the phones-away announcement, I silenced my phone and then dropped it into my bag by my foot. I sat in a dark room for the next hour and watched the Boston Rebels special teams. When the video session ended, we all rose, grabbed our stuff, and headed for the exit. There was no game tonight, so I planned on locking myself into my apartment to have my regrets over falling into bed with Jamie Hennessy.

"Hey, you got a second?" Oli called as we made our

way to the players' exit. The corridors were filled with team staff, some rolling carts of dirty towels to the laundry drop-off, and some hustling to the ice to lay down the wooden flooring required for a concert tonight. "Are you feeling good enough to grab a bite to eat?"

"I... sure, of course." I gave Oli a shaky smile.

"Great. Meet me at my place. Since we're partners, I want to talk to you about the charity hockey games starting next Summer."

"Already?"

"It's never too soon, and you did volunteer to do this with me."

"I know, I mean... no, I..." He folded his arms over his chest; one eyebrow raised, while I fell over myself trying to devise a reason not to go to his house to eat without sounding rude. "I just..." I threw a pleading look at Phillipe, but the tendie was deep in conversation with our goalie coach, and everyone else had cleared out in a rush.

"I know my place is kind of far out, but I'd like to spend time with the girls," he tacked on to be that guy. Shit.

"Of course, your house sounds great." I lied so big and badly they could have seen the glaring *LIAR* stamp on my forehead from the air traffic control tower at LAX.

"Cool, follow me. I think Jamie will be serving something light."

"Jamie. Light. Super. Yeah, yum."

Oliver trotted to the car. I schlepped to mine, threw my bag into the back of my new SUV, and then slid behind the wheel to sulk. Fuck. Okay, so this was doable. I had to be polite and smile at the man whose ass I'd ravaged then ran away from a mere twelve hours ago.

I should give up on men and sex and become a monk. Could monks play hockey? I'd check into it if I didn't die from embarrassment and shame in the next two hours.

Jamie seemed stunned to see me slide like a snake into the kitchen. His mouth fell open, and he fumbled to tug the loose-necked tee he was wearing up to his ears. Too late, though. I'd seen the marks I'd left on his pale skin. My dick reacted to seeing the dark love bites with a kick. Monkhood. Yep, I was looking into a life of quiet reflection and abstinence in some ivy-covered French monastery.

It's hard to play hockey for the Storm if you're picking lavender at an abbey in Provence.

Shit. Maybe the French monks had a hockey team. I'd research that as well.

"Hey, we have company for lunch," Oliver announced a bit too merrily. Jamie pasted on a smile that made his cheeks apple up so deeply I couldn't see his pretty eyes. "I hope you have enough for a guest?"

"Guest, yes, of course. We love guests." Jamie turned to the stove, turned the blue flame under a soup pot off, and faced his friend. "May I have a word with you in private, please?"

"Sure. Why don't you have a seat, Craig? We'll be a minute."

I nodded at Oli, sat at the table, and noticed no little girls. Huh, maybe they were upstairs napping. I wanted a long nap that would last until my flight to the monastery for hockey monks took off. I rubbed my knotted forehead to ease the furrows etched on it when Jamie's usually calm voice grew in intensity.

"What the fuck are you doing? Why the fuck did you bring him here for lunch?!"

Oh shit. I gauged the size of the window over the sink. No, not big enough for me to wiggle out of to make a sneaky escape. My phone buzzed. I should have left it in my bag, but no, I had to be an internet junkie. My sister's latest text about a dinner for my parent's fortieth anniversary in four months sat right above the one from Leon.

"We're partners in a hockey event next Summer benefitting the local LGBTQ teen shelter, and I wanted to talk strategy with him," Oliver replied.

"Strategy. For something happening next year?"

"Also, I wanted to see the girls."

"The girls are in school! You did this on purpose; admit it. I shouldn't have told you and Jackson about my mistake last night!"

Ouch. Wow, that hurt way more than it should. A mistake. Shit, that stung. But he was right. What we'd done had been a drunken mistake. It should and would never happen again. My past was littered with terrible blunders. The proof was a text on my phone from the last ghastly screwup I'd made.

"You should keep your voice down," Oliver said in a harsh whisper.

"Sod off. I'm not keeping my fucking voice down. I told you about that in confidence, and then you bring the man here. What on earth were you thinking?!"

"I was thinking you and him could patch things up. You look like you had a good time, and he's a great guy."

Aww, Oliver was so friendly. That made me feel good.

"Good guys do not ghost you in the middle of the night." And that made me feel like shit. "And not even a clean ghosting. No, he had to run into your damn boyfriend, who sleeps far too lightly for any normal human being!"

Oli snorted a laugh.

"Do *not* laugh at me. I'm fucking pissed at you for this, and I will *not* be making you lunch. So, you can take your sneaky but not sneaky charity partner to the fucking Arby's for all I care. I hope you choke on a curly fry!"

"Really?" Oliver asked weakly.

"No, but I hope you get acid reflux and burp all day."

With that, Jamie stormed up the stairs and slammed a door. His bedroom door, I had to assume. The same bedroom we'd torn up like two wild animals. My cock twitched at the memory of Jamie riding me, his cock bouncing, his ass clenched around my—

"Okay, so change of plan," Oliver said as he entered the kitchen, hands in his front pockets. "Jamie isn't up to cooking, so we'll head to a little Italian place I know nearby. They have great manicotti."

I pushed to my feet, bobbed my head, and followed Oliver outside. Jamie sat somewhere in that big house with the bikes in the yard, alone, hurt, and filled with regret. I longed to go back inside to talk to him about last night, but my heart warned me against it. It's better to let things end here. One ragged and painful cut now would heal quickly.

I hoped.

Chapter Five

Jamie

WOULD MY REACTION HAVE BEEN DIFFERENT IF, INSTEAD of staring at me like an idiot, Craig had immediately fallen to his knees and apologized for sneaking off? Maybe I wouldn't have been so irrational. Perhaps I would have pulled him into my arms, hugged him, and enjoyed more kisses.

But no, he stared at me in horror, and my hackles went up, and I got all prickly. Like some demented, threatened hedgehog.

I paced back and forth across my room, the restless energy of said hedgehog finally loosening its grip. He probably regretted sleeping with me, not that there had been much sleeping, and like me and any good Brit worth their weight in tea, he was being very un-American and avoiding the awkward situation. I needed to pull up my big boy's pants and get over myself.

I collapsed onto the bed, sprawling with limbs in every direction, and I lay staring at the ceiling as if it might offer some answers on dealing with the acute embarrassment of overreacting. Instead, my hand found my phone by habit, and before I knew it, I was unlocking it and tapping on Instagram. It wasn't my intention to check on Craig. I told myself it was just a scroll, just a way to pass the time.

But there I was, somehow ending up on the Storm's official page. One more tap, I was staring at a photo of Craig smiling broadly in the middle of a group of kids at some community event. The caption praised his ongoing commitment to a charity supporting dyslexia awareness, and the kids were grinning so hard I could feel their happiness in my chest. Craig wasn't only skilled on the ice; he was genuinely good, his actions speaking as loud as any of his game-winning goals.

I swiped on, my thumb mechanically moving while my mind raced. Another post, this time Craig at a local animal shelter, a small dog cradled in his arms, his expression soft and open. It wasn't just an image meant to tug at heartstrings for likes; it was real, it was him. Oli said he was kind and compassionate, so I had to believe he wasn't trying to hurt me by running and avoiding me. It had to be regret, that was all.

He regretted what we'd done on our drunken night of sex.

I needed to get over it and not take it so damn personally.

And as I lay there, the glow of my phone illuminating fragments of Craig's life, I couldn't help but whisper to myself, "Fuck my life."

I didn't want to get over it. I wanted to accidentally find myself in a situation where we had sex again and then talked and maybe even went out for a date. I'd take that in any order I could.

Somehow, I scrolled back on the Storm's social media, stopping at the announcement of Oli being traded in, and I recalled the moment he'd told me he was leaving New York to head west with the girls. I'd finally found a best friend, and I'd been so close to losing him, and there had never been any question I'd follow him here.

I wondered if Sean had known I would go wherever Oli and the girls went. I wondered if he had seen how much they were my family when I had none. Had I chased him away even before he stole my research and turned into a raging arsehole?

Fuck. Was him breaking my academic heart all my fault?

"Stop it," I told myself, forcing all that guilt and self-accusation back where it belonged, way down... *way* down. I hadn't forced Sean to steal my ideas; he'd done that himself. I hadn't forced him to fuck the intern with the mohawk over our sofa when he knew I was due home.

The following post was a throwback Thursday-type post, and front and center, set to some hip hop song (I think), was a montage of Craig and... wait... he could do handstands on the ice? In all his gear, and wait... that was him doing a pirouette and then sliding along the top of the boards on his ass, and spinning on the ice and...

"That is sexy," I told the room. I really needed to stop talking to my damn room. Hockey players were supposed to be stampeding about, shoving, and checking with force, right? Not being all light on their skates and spinning in circles.

I was rewatching the video for the second time—well, thirtieth probably, but who was counting—when the phone rang, and the video disappeared. When I saw who was calling, I reluctantly picked up, hoping my voice wouldn't hold the irritation of being disturbed.

"Dr. Hennessy, this is Barbara Millstone from the University Grants Commission," the voice on the other end introduced herself, all business and brisk efficiency. "I'm calling regarding the continuation of your funding for the research."

My heart sank. UCLA had been holding up the second installment of my funding, and without it, my research was as good as stalled. I knew Oli wouldn't kick me out of his house. I wasn't paying rent and didn't spend much money, but my reserves were running out, and I needed something to show for all my degrees.

"Yes, Ms. Millstone, I appreciate your call," I replied, trying to mask my anxiety with politeness.

"The committee has reviewed your initial findings, Dr. Hennessy. While they're academically intriguing, there's concern about their practical applications outside of academia. The committee suggests we need to see a tangible connection to real-world uses to continue funding."

Sean had taken nearly all my practical applications with him, leaving me with theories but nothing to show for them. I swallowed, the reminder of my stolen work in New York burning fresh in my memory. I needed anything that could tie mathematical principles' abstract beauty to everyday life's gritty reality.

As Ms. Millstone awaited my response, my thoughts

returned to Craig, spinning effortlessly on the ice, his body a perfect embodiment of grace through angles and spirals. Then inspiration struck—a vivid, sudden rush of possibility.

"Actually, Ms. Millstone, I've been developing a concept on how the Fibonacci sequence can be applied to predict and enhance performance in professional athletics," I exclaimed, my mind racing ahead of my words. "Particularly, I'm looking at applications in sports training and real-time performance analytics, which could revolutionize strategies and outcomes."

There was a pause, and I held my breath, hoping my impromptu idea sounded as promising aloud as it did in my head.

"That sounds... promising, Dr. Hennessy," she finally said, her tone shifting from skeptical to intrigued. "I will need a detailed outline of this proposal on my desk by midday on Friday. Can you manage that?"

I glanced at the calendar. I only had a few days to frame a hypothetical research application into a compelling grant proposal. "Yes, I can do that," I responded, a mixture of dread and excitement swirling within me.

"Very well," Ms. Millstone said. "We'll look forward to it. Good day, Dr. Hennessy."

As I hung up, the challenge sparked something—an eagerness, a purpose, and a reason to talk to the Storm, AKA Craig mostly, and maybe turn the debacle of our sexual encounter into something like a date. I turned back to the video of Craig; his movements were now a display of athletic prowess and a dance of numbers and possibilities. I could save my research with this new angle and add a new dimension.

I scrambled off my bed and threw the door open, stumbling down to the office Oli had given me free rein to use. I fell so hard into the chair that it rolled backward. Signing in took too long, but finally, I had all my research sources up and an empty document to start typing.

"Dynamic Patterns and Predictive Models: Integrating the Fibonacci Spiral and Chaos Theory in Sports Performance Optimization," I said as I typed, then backspaced a few times to ensure I was happy. I'd need to gather data, and I probably needed a football player, one of those with the funny-shaped balls like our rugby, who threw them a long way when they were spinning. Maybe a gymnast, and I needed a hockey player, maybe one who did spirals on the ice.

Hell. Who was I kidding?

This was me making plans to talk to Craig and get a date.

THE COACH'S OFFICE WAS CRAMPED AND CLUTTERED. IT was a small space dominated by a large, worn desk littered with play diagrams and performance reports. A whiteboard on one wall was packed with tactical notes and team rosters in various dry-erase markers. The air smelled of old coffee and the faint musk of sweat—a scent that seemed embedded into the very fabric of the place.

I sat in one of the two squeaky chairs opposite the couch, my hands clasped tightly in my lap to stop them from trembling. Coach stared across at me with a mix of curiosity and impatience, his bushy eyebrows furrowed. I'd already talked to team management, and they'd fobbed me off with a coach who, they said, would understand way more about my work than they did.

"So, what is this about, Dr. Hennessy?" he asked, leaning back in his chair, which creaked under his weight.

"Please call me Jamie," I said, then I cleared my throat, aware the explanation I had prepared might not bridge the gap between mathematical theory and ice hockey directly enough for him. "My research concerns the application of mathematical patterns—specifically, the Fibonacci spiral —and their manifestation in strategic plays in hockey. By analyzing the natural spiraling movements that players naturally employ during games, we can potentially enhance predictive modeling and training methods," I explained, my voice steady despite my inner tremor. "I suggested Craig Beaulieu because of his figure skating experience as a child, but I understand if he's not interested in working with me."

Coach Daniels stared at me, his expression unreadable for a long moment, and I wondered if he was seeing through the lie. Then, without a word, he blinked, his face settling into stunned confusion. "You lost me, but I'm a stats man, and if it helps the team, I'm all ears."

There was a knock, and the door opened, and Craig stepped in. He was dressed in his practice gear, a towel draped around his neck. His presence suddenly filled the small room, and awkward tension hovered between us— unspoken and heavy with the memory of that night.

"You wanted to see me, Coach?" Craig asked,

frowning. His eyes flicked briefly to mine before settling back on him. He was stiff and seemed worried, but I guess this was like being called into a principal's office. Maybe he thought he was in trouble.

Oh shit! Did he think I was in here talking about the sex? I shook my head at him, and his frown deepened. Did I say something? Did I reassure him before he started defending what we did and—

"Jamie here was just telling me about some... math stuff. Spirals in hockey or something," Coach said, waving a hand vaguely in my direction. He turned to Craig. "I'm getting coffee, and I'll let him explain it to you directly."

Craig nodded, shifting his gaze back to me. His eyebrows raised in silent invitation to continue as soon as Coach ambled off.

"This wasn't about the sex," I exclaimed.

Craig winced, his gaze not meeting mine for a moment. "Okay, and?"

"We can forget about the sex; I mean, I don't want to because it was delicious, and your cock was perfect and... shit..." I placed a hand over my mouth as Craig's lips twitched. "Focus, Jamie," I muttered, then took a deep breath. "Craig, I'm working on a research project that involves the application of the Fibonacci sequence and chaos theory in sports. Specifically, I believe that your on-ice movements, particularly your skating patterns that echo your childhood training as a figure skater, could provide valuable data for predictive analytics in sports training," I tried to sound as confident as possible.

Craig listened, his expression thoughtful. "Okay... and what do you need from me?"

"About ten hours of your time spread out according to what suits your schedule. I want to record some of your practice sessions, talk about your figure skating past, and possibly discuss your experiences and thoughts about your movements and decisions during games."

Craig considered this for a moment, then nodded slowly. "You just want to watch?"

"Yep."

"I don't have to write anything, study, or…"

"Nope."

"Okay, then. Let me know the dates and times, and we'll sort it out," Craig replied, standing as if he were going to leave.

"Can I have your number?" I blurted, and he stared at me. "For fixing dates and things."

"Ask Oli to add you to our chat or a new chat."

"I will."

"Okay then."

"Okay."

He hesitated at the door, then turned to me and leaned down. His lips were *this close* to my ear. He smelled of sweat and yuck and exercise, but fuck, it was good.

"That was one of the hottest hookups of my entire life," he whispered and left.

Holy hell.

I was hard and shaky because Craig was a potent mix of every chemical and physical thing that turned me on.

I had to stop myself from calling him back.

Chapter Six

Craig

I HAD BARELY EXITED THE COACH'S OFFICE WHEN MY brain finally got a tight hold on the situation. My feet stalled next to a snack machine.

That had been one of the hottest hookups of my entire life.

"Stupid, stupid, triple stupid," I growled softly then thunked my forehead into the glass of the snack machine. Four times. On the fifth *thunk* a bag of cheesy puffs fell to the tray. I took them, shoved two bucks into the tray, and ripped the bag open. What I needed now was comfort food and a swift kick in the ass. I shoved handfuls of cheesy goodness into my mouth, chewing aggressively, my thoughts a whirlwind. When would I learn? When would my stupid dick stop shoving into normal conversations with beautiful, smart men? Why did I do these things?

A soft clearing of a throat stole into the beatdown of

myself. I jerked my head from the glass of the snack machine, spun, and found myself staring at Jamie. Had he gotten better-looking since I'd left him five minutes ago? Impossible. Yet not. His tie was a thin blue one that made his eyes sparkle and glow.

"Hey," I coughed out, sending orange powder into the air.

One side of his mouth twitched. "Enjoying those, are you?"

"Yeah, I always eat cheesy doodles after a workout." Damn it. That was a secret. No one should know about my cheesy doodle fixation. If the team dietician found out he would roast me like a sesame seed. But I had blurted it out because my mouth seemed to think that was something clever to say.

"I call them Wotsits," he announced with a nose wrinkle and then walked off. My gaze fell on his tight ass in those sexy khakis. An ass I'd ravaged at his request. An ass I would give up this bag of snacks and any future cheese puffs to sink into again. He glanced back just once, a lurid glance over a shoulder that screamed *Follow me for more delights* and I took two steps before common sense arrived to slap me in the face.

"I need help," I mumbled, shoved four Cheetos into my mouth, and jogged off to find a quiet place to call my sister. The video room was empty, so I ducked inside, flipped on the lights, saw a bright orange handprint on the switch, and then used my elbow to wipe it clean. My ass found a chair in front, the seat creaking as I sat. I wiped my fingers on my hoodie then pulled my phone out of the front pocket. I could care less if I had big streaks of cheese dust on my purple Storm hoodie. This was an emergency. I hit Claudia's contact button for a video call. No way in hell was I trying to type out the chaos in my head. I waited and ate more cheesy treats as the call rang through. When she picked up my cheeks were full. She pulled on her glasses —little wire-framed ones like John Lennon used to wear— and sighed dramatically.

"What's going on now?" she asked, the sound of her cute little voice making me feel less panicked.

"So, there's this man…"

"*Craig…*"

"I know." I pushed two doodles into my face and chewed then swallowed. "I'm so stupid."

"You are *not* stupid. When it comes to men you're just easily cock-blinded but otherwise you're damn smart. So, first stop using the S-word for yourself. You know we do not allow that word to be anywhere near us."

I loved her to bits. She was a little bitty thing, like a sprite or a pixie, with brown curls and chocolate eyes like mine. We'd been quite a good skating pair. I could fling her around with ease as she weighed less than my hockey bag. Neither of us had planned to make careers out of figure skating, so when I'd switched to hockey my sister had done solo for a few years and then went to college. She still skated recreationally when she could find the time. Claudia worked for a women's charity now, was single and loving it, and had a Chinese Crested Dog named Bruno.

Actually, Bruno was my dog. Leon had given him to

me for our first anniversary and it had been love at first sight for me. Sadly, because of the break-up, Claudia was now his guardian. She loved him as much as I did and spoiled him rotten. Even though I knew he was in a good home I still missed him. Bruno and I had spent more than one night curled up together, him licking my face as I battled with tears and crushing self-doubt after a vicious verbal flailing from my ex.

I spoke to Bruno for a few minutes, him sat on Claudia's lap, and then he trotted off to sunbathe. I could relate to how Oliver felt having to leave his most precious possessions with someone else while he played hockey.

I'd felt terrible leaving him with her at first, but my travel schedule was terrible from September through June. My sister worked from home most of the time and was much better suited for a dog in terms of hours spent with the little stinker. I took over in the summer, spending my off time with her and Bruno hidden away in a small town in Michigan.

Hidden hopefully being the key word.

Because Leon wanted Bruno back—not because he loved Bruno, but because he wanted to hurt me.

"What's the second thing?"

"Whoever this brainiac loser is, distance yourself from him now." I couldn't meet her eyes. "Oh, Craig."

"I know. I really didn't mean to fall into this intellectual man trap again." I waved my orange fingers in the air. "He's just so cute, and smart, damn he's smart. He uses words that I have to Google like they were sprinkles on ice cream."

"Craig..."

"And he's funny. And British! You know I love foreign men."

"Craig…"

"And he's sexy. So sexy. He wears waistcoats like someone from a Jane Austen book. Like Mr. Darcy! You love Mr. Darcy. *I* love Mr. Darcy!"

"Craig…"

My lips were sticky with cheese dust but that didn't seem to slow the rush of words flowing past them.

"And yes, we might have hooked up a few nights back. And yes, it might have been the best sex ever, and yes I totally freaked out and ghosted him but now I'm wondering if I shouldn't have pulled that Casper routine because I still want to do him and maybe get to know him better while we—"

"Craig!" The verbal onslaught skidded to a halt. "We are *not* doing this again. That is what you told me after Leon broke you into tiny bits. You told me to remind you of all the nasty shit that big-brained jerk did to you if you ever found yourself in this situation again."

"I know but…"

"You told me to step in and virtually or physically slap you if you ever even *winked* at a man with several degrees."

"I know but…"

"Craig Lewis Beaulieu, do not make me fly over from Michigan."

Man, for being so petite she was not one to be trifled with. "I won't."

"Good, then when we talk next I'll be seeing you

without the telltale signs of man problems all over your chin, right?"

I wiped the back of my hand over my lips and chin. Oo, cheesy. "You're going to distance yourself from this guy before he can sink his academic claws into you, right?" I needed another bag. "You'll not see this man in any way, shape, or form. Right?"

"Hmm, oh, right. Well, no, not right. I kind of agreed to work with him on a science project about spirals and sports."

I winced at the huge, profane blast from such a sweet little woman. This call was going to be a lot longer—and louder—than I had expected. I totally needed more cheesy doodles.

The next few days were filled with worry and puffed cheese treats.

I'd eaten so many cheesy doodles I was beginning to fret over looking jaundiced. My mother liked to tell the story about when I was a baby I'd eaten so many bowls of strained carrots and squash over several months that she and my father thought I was jaundiced. That was going to be me soon. Craig Beaulieu, the pumpkin-faced player. I had no clue what Jamie was going to do to me in our first session. Maybe he would tie me down to a lab table and poke me with needles. No, that would be mean. Maybe he would tie me down to a lab table and have his way with me. He'd come in wearing a white lab coat and nothing else, then after I was secured to the gurney he would toss his lab coat aside but keep those sexy-as-sin glasses on as he climbed over me and sat on my cock. I'd be naked too, obviously.

"Hey, Booboo, you are drooling on the ice."

I crashed back to real life as the sound of Vlad Novikov's thickly accented Russian taunt tickled my ear. I threw a glower at the man they called Iceberg for his cold demeanor. He knew I hated him calling me Booboo. The dumb Arizona Raptor always got in my face. Why did we have to play them so frequently?

"Fuck off."

"Oh, such a clever tongue you have, Booboo." Iceberg chuckled roughly before nudging me aside to pick up the puck that his boyfriend Tate Collins had won in the faceoff. Sure, the Russian was big, but I had speed. I juked around him at center ice, stole the puck by lifting his stick, and passed it to our captain who took a quality shot at goal on Colorado Penn. The Raptors fans cheered the nice save by their rock-star goalie as we went back to the bench for a TV timeout. We'd flown into Tucson last night, had a nice light practice this morning, and spent a few hours in the desert. I'd been told the heat and sand would calm me, but it didn't. All it did was make me sweat and burn the back of my neck. When we returned to LA in three days—we had a quick trip down to Dallas for a game—Jamie would be waiting to do things to me. With me. With. Me.

I seriously needed to get my shit together. It was the middle of the season, and we were in third place. We needed every point we could get. Porn-dreaming about a scientist on the ice was going to get me benched for sure. Coach was not pleased with my plus-minus numbers over the past couple of games. I'd been on the ice for four goals against. Not good. And it was all because of Jamie

Hennessy and his lab coat. Did he even wear one? And if not, if I asked would he consider it?

"Nice defensive work on Novikov," our new associate coach, Mike Trayson, said as he pounded on my shoulder pads. Mike was a good guy, firm but kind, with a solid background coaching both the pros and minor league teams. "That's what we like to see. Speed and determination."

"Thanks, Coach," I panted, taking a mouthful of water then rinsing my mouth free of the lactic acid build-up. I spat on the mat between my skates. "He's tough."

"You're tougher," Mike shouted to be heard over the roar of the crowd after Cam and Colorado had a knot-up in the Arizona goalie's space.

Penn was now shoving Cameron. The Raptors were flying into the crease to defend their goalie. The Storm blew into the zone as well. A fist flew and the refs dove into the melee. Both teams were on their feet in their respective boxes beating on the boards with our sticks.

The donnybrook lasted a few seconds. The refs spent several minutes divvying up penalty minutes. When things were calm both teams had a man in the sin bin for roughing.

Cam and Tate were still mouthing off at each other as we hit the ice, four a side, which was always a fun two minutes. The ice was bigger.

Pierre was shouting something at us in French when the faceoff went to his right instead of on my stick. I chased it down, turned, and shot to the left to avoid a bruising bodycheck from a big man in a red jersey.

"Man on!" Pierre yelled to let me know I had a defender on my ass as I streaked behind his goal.

I dug in hard in the corner, moved left and then right to shake off the bigger and slower D-man, and raced down the ice to take a shot on Penn. It hit his shoulder, flew into the air, and was flipping end over end until the puck dropped behind the Raptors tendie. I shoved my stick behind Penn who was on his knees, head twisting to try to locate that round rubber disc. The edge of my stick just brushed the puck. Someone came in hard behind me, a wrecking ball of solid muscle knocking me off my skates. I went down hard.

The red light behind Penn flared to life. I scrambled up, met my teammates in the corner, and had a nice little celly while Iceberg cleared the puck from the Raptors net. Penn was arguing with the ref, his helmet thrown to the ice, about goaltender interference I assumed. But the Raptors coaches didn't dispute the goal and Penn eventually went back to his crease but spent the rest of the game slapping me with his paddle if I got within range. Which was fine. I was used to goalies poking at or pushing me. Pierre did the same thing, with way more flair and lots of French cussing, so it was to be expected.

We left Arizona with two points. The flight to Dallas was short and choppy. I disliked turbulence of any kind, but thankfully, I had an audio book to keep me distracted from the bouncing and flashes of lightning as we circled Dallas/Fort Worth. Landing was postponed due to the storm so here we sat, going in circles, which felt kind of fitting since that night I'd had wild sex with Jamie. I couldn't shake the man from my thoughts no matter how I tried or how many times Claudia told me to. It wasn't as easy as my sister wanted it to be, that was for sure. He was there all the time. When I slept, when I woke up, on the ice, off the ice. The memories of our night in bed replayed repeatedly whenever I closed my eyes.

I struggled to keep the man out of my head during games.

Water streaked the window. My book played on, but I wasn't listening to it.

My mind was on this scientific thing with Jamie. I should have refused. Should've just said nope and moved on with my life. Now I was stuck. I felt someone watching me. My gaze flitted around the charter jet to find Oli staring at me. I nodded. He smiled. We were friends, Oli and I, and he knew everything about that night. He'd never mentioned it or hinted about what he thought of me sleeping with his best friend.

Or not sleeping, as the case may be.

He'd never again tried to interfere with the two of us and the tangled mess of whatever it was we were doing. Maybe he assumed that was personal, or maybe Jamie had told him to never discuss it. Probably so. That would be the wisest.

To remind myself of how wise pretending to have sex with Jamie was, I paused my book, opened my texts, and made sure my headphones were connected because fuck if I wanted anyone hearing this shit. I had my phone read the latest one from Leon that had arrived just last night. The computer voice lessened the harshness of the words, but they still cut me deep, and god knows why I kept them.

Why are you being so stupid, Craig? Don't make me

get litigious. Come back to me, and I won't take this further. Call me. Soon. L

My exhalation was shaky. I closed my phone, leaving the text to sit with all the others Leon had sent me since I'd left him. Fuck him and his threats and his demands for me to go back to him. All I took the night I left was what was mine.

He'd called me stupid all the time.

And he'd said it again.

Chapter Seven

Jamie

THE YOUNG MAN ON THE END OF THE SOFA WAS CALLED Ian, a quarterback for the UCLA Pioneers in his final year of a degree in physics, and already drafted to enter the Seattle NFL team. He was incredibly bright, but I got the feeling he played at being a jock a little too well. He was tall, wiry, fast, and he brought a ball with him that he balanced on his hand and spun when he was thinking.

The woman next to him was Annabelle, an artistic gymnast, also in her last year at UCLA with a near-finished chemistry degree, already training for the Olympic gymnastics team, who was sitting so still I wondered if she was meditating. The only thing that kept her attention was Ian and his flirting, and only when he was trying really hard. The two of them shared the small two-seater sofa. Ian was sprawling and posturing and balancing the ball, and Annabelle was side-eyeing him and smiling.

I guessed there could be an Annabelle/Ian matchup happening soon.

I took the seat opposite Craig and glanced around the empty room, feeling proud that I'd found this quiet space within the bustle of the college and had managed to book it even though I wasn't an assistant professor here.

Yet.

I had reasons to stay in LA, particularly now Oli had implied over beers last night that he'd retire before being traded away from LA and from Jackson. Not to mention the girls loved their new school. He was putting down roots in LA, actively researching a bigger place for him, Jackson, and the girls, with an extra room for me, apparently.

So, if he and the girls were staying, then I was too.

The walls were adorned with whiteboards covered in a myriad of notes and diagrams from countless meetings before us, lending an academic yet comforting air to the place, and I felt calm and collected and in control of my research. More than when it had been Sean and me doing this together, when he would flutter around as if he knew what he was doing.

Craig had followed me in reluctantly, his discomfort palpable as his sight flicked rapidly between the boards and the seats. "You sure this is a good spot?" he'd asked, voice laced with skepticism as he glanced around the lounge, clearly out of his element among the scribbles of quantum mechanics and organic chemistry. I bet he'd be better with all those X's and O's of strategy, but I hoped he'd learn to love my world as well.

God knows why that was important to me.

He was just a hookup.

One night.

One sexy, awe-inspiring, memory-making night.

"It's relaxed, and we've got coffee," I'd tried to reassure him, gesturing to the small bar where the machine sat with the pods I'd stolen from Oli's kitchen.

He hadn't seemed convinced but settled into a lone chair anyway, placing a Storm hoodie in his lap as a makeshift barrier, and looked every bit the solitary figure, set slightly apart from Ian and Annabelle, who were so deep into their flirtatious banter I wondered if they needed to find another kind of room for privacy.

Ian was all confidence and charm, a glaring contrast to Craig's reserve. He tossed his football lightly from one hand to the other, catching it and spinning it occasionally as he spoke. "Physics is all about understanding the forces of attraction, much like the one I'm feeling right now," he said, winking at Annabelle, who raised an eyebrow, her posture poised and composed. She seemed amused by Ian, but every now and then, her gaze would cut to Craig, and she'd try to catch his eye.

Mine.

Craig watched them both, and then his gaze swung back to me, eyes clouding with an unreadable emotion. I could tell he was out of his comfort zone when his hands tightened around the purple material he'd folded and refolded, and he leaned back, trying to appear casual but only managing to present a picture of contained energy. He wore a Storm T-shirt that clung just right to his lithe, muscular frame, accentuating the build of a professional hockey player honed by years on the ice. His jeans were casual, and his purple Converse were adorned with the Storm logo, another nod to his team spirit. His brown hair was a tousled mess, with waves and flicks and curls that looked like they had been styled by his carefree movements rather than a deliberate effort, and he was so gorgeous.

I couldn't help but notice the smoothness of his clean-shaven jaw, which made him appear young—vulnerable almost—and so damn handsome. A vivid sense memory flashed through my mind—of the faint abrasion of his stubble against my skin—and boom, I was fighting getting an erection in the middle of an academic meeting. I went through the entire lengthy theorem before I had myself under control, and realized he was staring at me, or rather I was staring at him, and he'd caught me.

He seemed slightly on edge, sitting with one leg crossed over the other, occasionally adjusting the material in his lap or running fingers through his hair. I wondered if sitting still was something foreign to him. What would he do while I was sitting reading? Would he go to the gym? Watch a movie? Would he want to talk? Would he hate that when we were in our house one day sometimes I needed to sit in silence, or would he curl up next to me and read something himself?

Also, why was I picturing us on a lazy afternoon in a non-existent house, in a non-starting relationship, with the sexy man staring at me?

I sent him a hesitant smile, and he returned it, although it didn't seem entirely genuine. Maybe he could read my mind, saw my future-us imaginings, and was completely freaked out.

I caught myself fantasizing about leaning close to him, drawn by the magnetic pull of his presence. The thought of kissing him sent a familiar warmth coursing through me, mingled with a pang of longing. The small room was filled with Ian and Annabelle's chatter, but for a moment, it all seemed to fade into the background, leaving only the vivid image of Craig, his casual beauty, and the unresolved tension between us.

I wanted him.

So badly.

My watch buzzed with the alarm to start the meeting, and I snapped into motion.

"Hi, everyone, thank you for coming. We'll start in a bit, but I just thought we'd go around the room and give ourselves an idea of who we are." Craig sunk lower in his seat—I got that this meeting warm-up was shit, I hated doing it myself, but I needed everyone to understand what they were here to do, and this was the best way.

"I'll go first," Ian announced, and that didn't surprise me at all. "I'm Ian, QB for the Lions, Go Lions!" He held up a fist—was he expecting me to bump it?

"Go Lions," I repeated, and he seemed happy.

"So, I'm in the final year of my degree, physics, but I'm already on the books for the Seattle Sirens, so I'm pretty set for life."

Unless he got injured, in which case he wasn't set at all, but I didn't want to burst his bubble.

"I'm Annabelle, last year, Chemistry, and I have my place on the Olympic team." She glanced at Ian who seemed suitably impressed. "Plus, a post-grad at Cambridge. England I mean, not US."

Then it was Craig's turn, and I smiled in encouragement as he cleared his throat.

"Craig, winger, LA Storm, hockey."

"And I'm Dr Jamie Hennessy, call me Jamie, and I want to thank the three of you for coming today."

All three of them mumbled a hello.

"So, uh, this place is full of... equations and stuff," Craig finally commented, his attempt at making conversation falling a bit flat as he gestured vaguely toward the nearest whiteboard laden with complex calculations. "I thought this was a physical thing."

"Yeah, it's a bit different from the ice rink or the field, isn't it?" I responded, trying to bridge the gap between his world and this one. "But hey, it's a change of scenery. Good for the brain."

He offered a half-smile, still tense. "Sure, as long as I don't have to solve any of that," he said, nodding at the boards.

"That's my job," I reassured him, and Craig seemed relieved. I wasn't expecting anyone here to understand what I was doing from a mathematical perspective, and I wanted Craig to relax, and what I said seemed to work. "So, the basic question I was asking in my research was about the orientation of flight. Take for example, a football." Ian perked up. "It starts with the nose up but then tilts forward by the time it reaches the receiver."

"Are you talking about that professor who reached rotation precesses?"

"Exactly, everyone thought the spin was similar to a spinning top's behavior—gyroscopic stability and all that. But it's constantly interacting with air currents, which alter its spin axis dynamically, so..." I thought I'd let Ian finish for the ultimate teachable moment.

"Airflow creates a dynamic torque on the ball. The spiral isn't just stable spinning; it's a dynamic system responding to continuous external torques like gyroscopic precession." He elbowed Annabelle. "The external torque due to air modifies the spin axis, making it precess. The football's axis makes a cone shape around the direction of motion. This is why the nose tilts down toward the end of the pass." He sat back, waiting for her to be impressed, which she seemed to be at first, and then the two started chatting back and forth about theoretical calculations and computer simulations to prove the behavior. That gave me time to stare at Craig, who in turn was staring at the boards, pale. Did he not feel well? We could always reschedule if he was coming down with something.

Ian finally turned back to me. "So, you're giving us a perfect example of how theoretical physics applies to everyday phenomena, and you want to use math in the same way?"

"Maths," I corrected.

Ian frowned. "Math," he repeated.

"Maths," I sighed with added drama. "Maths is short for mathematics, hence the extra s."

Ian wrinkled his nose. "Is that like a Brit thing?"

I held back the sarcasm and smiled, pretty used to the banter. "Not, it's like a word thing."

Ian snickered and shook his head. "You Brits really like to add extra letters, huh? Next thing you'll tell me is that color needs a *U* or something."

I noticed Craig shooting the kid a sharp glance, but Annabelle beat Craig to whatever he was going to say.

"Rude," she huffed and elbowed the boy, and

something in her admonishment made Ian sit straighter—jeez, he wanted to impress her something bad.

"Sorry, sir, doctor, Jamie," Ian fumbled.

"It's okay. So back to what I was saying, uhm, understanding these principles could definitely give you all an edge, knowing exactly how to control the pass more effectively in football, understanding the geometry of the spiral in hockey, or the gravitational force applied to a set of gymnastic movements. So, let's get started."

I handed out the clipboards with the questionnaire. Craig took his as if it were an unexploded bomb, placing it on his lap on top of the hoodie.

"What I need from you is a baseline of your understanding of spirals, just single words is fine, how it might help you to control your movements on a mathematical basis."

Ian was already scribbling, Annabelle, reading the form thoroughly. It was only a few pages, the usual questions, names, health and safety forms, and then some aims for their participation and what they hoped to gain from it.

Craig hadn't shifted from his initial frozen posture since receiving the clipboard. "I'll do this at home, Dr. Hennessy," he said finally, his voice firm yet quiet.

"Please, call me Jamie," I reminded him, and he stared at me. I was puzzled by his reaction. "It's okay, I know it's a lot of boxes, it's really not meant to be detailed. Just a few questions that help us understand your thoughts on what I need to achieve."

He shook his head, eyes not meeting mine. "I'll handle it at home."

His response left me confused. "It's really straightforward, Craig. Nothing you need to really think about. You can leave the aims bit if you like," I pressed, not understanding his reluctance.

Craig stood abruptly. The clipboard and hoodie tumbled to the floor, but he didn't seem to notice. "I appreciate you asking me to be part of this, Jamie, but I have to step out of this study," he said calmly, his voice carrying a finality that stopped me short.

I watched, stunned, as he strode toward the door without another word. A mixture of shock and concern propelled me after him. "Craig! Wait, is this because of—because we had sex?" The question was out before I could reel it back, and I glanced at Ian and Annabelle who were staring with mouths open. Fuck. Had I just outed him? Fuck. "Only joking," I added lamely, but it was too late, and I'd seriously fucked up.

He turned to face me, with an unreadable expression, although he didn't look furious, merely disappointed. He glanced left and right then grabbed my arm and encouraged me down the corridor and into a stairwell. "Dr. Hennessy—"

"Jamie, please, and god, I didn't mean to out you—"

"It's not that, and it's nothing to do with us having sex." He cradled my face and backed me against the wall. "That part of my life works great," he murmured, and for a second I thought he was going to kiss me. Instead, he tugged my face to his and rested his forehead against mine.

"I don't belong in there. I have dyslexia. I can't read the form quickly like everyone else, and I have software that reads it, and special... look, I'm not stupid, but I'm not academic," he explained, his voice low but resolute. "I thought you knew."

The realization hit me like a punch to the gut. Here was Craig, strong and confident in so many ways, confronting a challenge that went largely unseen by those around him, and I hadn't known. I never even thought about making my study open to everyone, I assumed with him being an athlete that he'd be...

What?

"I didn't realize," I managed to say, feeling utterly inadequate.

Craig gave a small smile, and he didn't seem sad, or angry. "It's just who I am. I know my strengths, Jamie, and that..." he gestured vaguely back toward the room, "that's not one of them."

"I can make it accessible."

"I know you can, but maybe that's not what I need from you."

"I don't understand."

"I don't need you to make allowances for me, I need to be..." He seemed frustrated. "I've been in a situation like this before..."

"In a scientific study?"

He snorted a laugh. "No, with a guy who made me think less of myself. I won't let it happen again, however much I want to kiss you."

"I didn't mean to... shit... Craig?"

"Bye."

Watching him walk away, I felt a profound respect mixed with my confusion. He was right; he knew his strengths and wasn't afraid to acknowledge his limitations.

But had I inadvertently pushed him into a situation that made him uncomfortable? This question gnawed at me as I stood in the hallway, the echo of the closing door at the end of the corridor ringing softly in the background.

It hadn't even crossed my mind to consider accessibility, and as a consequence, I'd made him think less of himself.

Talk about a mess.

Bloody hell.

Chapter Eight

Craig

"Hé! Hé! Hé! I am on your team, yes?!" Pierre shouted from the net. I lowered my stick as the irritated yell cut through the fog in my head. "What are you doing?! Trying to take off my head from my shoulders?" Our morning practice on Calgary ice fell into a stilted silence. I blinked at my teammate in the net and felt my face flame. "You head, eez vinegar there!"

I had no idea what that meant, but then Pierre had an interesting turn of phrase that not everyone followed.

"Sorry, I was… I don't know what you said there at the end," I replied, shamefaced, as Pierre whipped his mask off to glower at me. His face was so pretty that even a dark look seemed less of a glare and more of a pout, but those eyes of his were intense.

He skated out of his crease to get sweaty nose to sweaty nose with me. Not a soul on skates said a word but

I could feel every eye on the two of us. Man, this Canadian road trip was not going well at all for me.

"Your head fills with pickle juice. Whatever eez inside your skull making you fuck up is needing to be dumped into the sink. I am done!"

With that he stormed off the ice, leaving his mask, paddle, and blocker lying at his net. I shrunk into my jersey, wishing I could pull all the way in to hide like a turtle. Pierre was right. I'd been off for a solid week now, scattered and unable to focus, my play sloppy. My plus/minus had taken a nose dive over the past three games. I'd been solely responsible for a turnover that had led to a goal in our last game in Edmonton. If not for a squeaker goal from Cam in overtime we would have lost that game, and the tightness in our division meant every point counted.

"He'll cool off. You know his temper flares hot then dies off just as fast," Oli said from my right.

I bobbed my head, unable to speak, and worked up enough dignity to finish practice. Coach pretty much just sent us to the showers, his gaze on me as I slunk off like a dog caught with the Easter ham in his mouth. I picked up Pierre's equipment before heading to the locker room. I found our goalie standing in the corridor in only his hockey pants. He'd been staring at a mural on the wall while holding a can of grape soda. His dark eyes narrowed as I lumbered to him, goalie gear held out in front of me like a gift from a visiting dignitary trying to appease an upset king.

"Why is this coming to me from you?" He popped the

tab on his soda, sending fizz and purple foam over his fingers. "Putain!"

"I wanted to bring them in and apologize."

He glanced up, thick lashes framing dark chocolate eyes, as he licked grape soda from his fingers. "And why is this?" He lowered his hand from his lips as his sharp stare sliced into me. "Is there a bomb inside my blocker that will BOOM to take off my head since your practice shooting failed to decapitate me?"

"What? No, of course not. I felt bad for being distracted and wanted to bring you your paddle and stuff." I shoved the mound of gear at his chest. He sipped his soda, a standard refueling drink for him after every practice or game. The man had a thing for grape soda. Not that I was judging. Cheesy doodles called to me from my hotel room. I had purchased the party-size bag at a Safeway five minutes from where we were staying. "Look, I know I've been a putz of late."

"Explains what is this 'putz'." He let me stand there, stinky goalie gear in my arms, while he sipped soda like some sort of hockey emperor looking down upon a poor subject begging for forgiveness for a heinous crime.

"Oh, uhm, a putz is a Yiddish term for someone who's stupid."

His eyebrows knitted. "Non, you are not stupid." He knew all about my dyslexia. I'd never hidden it from the team. "Usually. Hmm, no, that is not what I meant. I mean your brain is not stupid because of the learning disability."

"Thanks."

"You are welcome. Give me my gear. Do not shoot fiery slapshots at me with intent to kill on your face again or I will soak your cup in grape soda and place it into the sun for drawing ants."

I shuddered at the mere thought. "Damn, is that a Quebecois punishment?"

"Non, we are sweet and gentle peoples. I just made it up." He handed me his empty can. "Go sort your head." He tugged his stuff from my arms and then disappeared into the dressing room, leaving me to find a recycle bin. Seemed I had some head-sorting to do if I wanted to avoid ants in my cup. That was easier said than done since I had no clue what was wrong.

Liar. You know what's wrong. You bailed on Jamie for something that was an innocent misunderstanding. What you're feeling is guilt, sparky.

Sadly, I couldn't argue with myself. I was right. I did feel bad for leaving Jamie high and dry over something that he could have no way known about me. I was a heel. I schlepped into the dressing room to peel off my sodden gear and shower. Somehow, I had to wheedle my way back into Jamie's good graces. I wanted him as a friend.

You want him for more than a friend.

"Okay, enough from me today," I grumbled to myself.

Charlie tossed me a worried look I waved off before dashing into the showers. I pretended not to see the other guys soaping and shampooing when they grunted hello as I passed.

Head down, eyes on your feet. That was queer kid rule number one in any locker room/community shower. I'd learned that lesson early. It had only taken one older kid hitting me to ensure I never glanced at a guy's junk in the showers ever again. Funny how assumptions had been made about me as a child. I'd never really presented as femme in any way, but because I was a figure skater, that made me gay. The bullshit stereotypes had clung hard until I'd made the switch to hockey. Then, because I was now playing a "manly" sport, I was no longer gay. Ha, ha. Guess what, haters. I was still just as queer if I were wearing skates with toe picks or without.

I found an empty stall. Oli stood on my left, focused on me while I placed my soap and shampoo on the tiled shelf and then cranked on the taps.

"Want to grab something to eat before we rest?" Oli asked all matter-of-fact. I was grateful for that. I didn't want to rehash the dressing down I'd recently gotten from our tendie.

"I could eat," I replied before shoving my head into a blast of hot water.

"Cool."

That was the entire conversation until we were seated at a smoky steakhouse with views of the Bow River. The steakhouse was hopping, every table filled with hungry patrons. I sat idly staring out at the river flowing through Calgary, a cold glass of water in front of me, my salad mostly untouched.

"People say that I'm a good listener if you'd like to talk about what's bothering you," Oli said as a server rushed by with two platters holding plump, rare steaks. My stomach growled at the sight. An early lunch filled with protein and veggies. Probably a better choice than a six-pack of soda and a party-size bag of cheesy doodles. "Well, Jackson says it, and so do the girls, if that matters."

I gave him a sad smile then speared a chunk of red pepper dripping with Italian dressing from my salad bowl.

"Yeah, it totally counts." I chewed and swallowed, using the brief pause to "*sort my head*," to quote Pierre. "Okay, so you probably know what happened at the college with the study that Jamie is heading."

"I've heard a little bit, yes," he replied cautiously.

"Did he tell you that I acted like a jerk?" Our steaks arrived, two huge T-bones, medium rare, with seasoned potato wedges and broccoli florets. Our server left us with some steak sauce and a fresh basket of wheat rolls. Once the cheery young lady in a bright blue apron scurried off, Oli plucked a bun from the basket and tore it in half.

"He said nothing about anyone being a jerk other than himself," he answered, then dipped his bun into the meaty juices leaking from his T-bone.

"Oh shit, I was hoping he wouldn't blame himself." I sighed over my steaming broccoli.

"He's British. They always blame themselves for everything," he tossed out with a knowing little smile. "Look, I know things kind of got off on a bad foot…"

"It was all me. Both feet, terribly bad. I overreacted to something unintentional. I thought I was old enough to not get hurt when I felt slow or dumb—"

"Craig, you are *not* dumb."

"I know, thank you, though. It's just a knee-jerk reaction. It's like if you're a chubby kid or a kid with crooked teeth or whatever sets you apart from the so-called norm as a child, then as an adult, you lose weight or get crowns or learn how to navigate the written word well enough to graduate college." I forked a floret and lifted it into the air to stare at it. "In your head, you know you've overcome whatever adversity you may have faced and have triumphed, but in your heart, in the tiny space left over from childhood where the mean words hurt, you just have this flash of pain that makes you flinch. I flinched way too hard. Jamie didn't know. How could he have? And I reacted as little Craig crying to his mom that the kids called him retarded."

"Craig, speaking as a parent, I fully understand how hard it can be on kids. My girls have gone through some pretty nasty things, snide and hurtful comments, and not always from other children. Adults can be callous. Hell, as queer men we know all too well the nasty that flows down over us on the daily."

"Amen," I sighed, then dipped my floret into a small cup of melted butter. "But Jamie wasn't mean, callous, or hateful. He was just doing what most people did. He assumed."

"Yes, and he feels awful."

I knew he did. He'd texted and called a dozen times over the past several days. I'd ignored them all because I was at first too hurt, then too embarrassed to answer him. "If you would reply to him, it might help with your inability to focus."

I nodded, unsure of how to go about opening up a conversation with the man after my bratty display. I picked up my steak knife and began cutting the charbroiled meat into small cubes. A few moments of quietude fell over our table while we dove into our food. The meat was tender and juicy, the potatoes coated with a garlic sauce that paired perfectly with the beef, and the broccoli was steamed to perfection.

I took a break to wipe my chin with a blue fabric napkin. Oli was chewing away merrily, his gaze meeting mine over the salt and pepper shakers in the center of our square table.

"If I were to try to apologize, what would be the best way?" I dared to ask and got a confused look. "Does he like flowers? Candy?"

"Oh." He placed his fork on the edge of his plate as he swallowed then took a drink of ice water. "Well, honestly, I don't think you need to buy him anything. And I don't think either of you owe each other an apology. Misunderstandings happen. Maybe you could call him and say you'd like to start over? That is if you're still interested in being in the study."

"I feel I need to give it another go. I ran out on it, and that's not me. I don't just bolt when something unpleasant happens. I fight harder."

"I know; I've seen that in you every time you're on the ice."

"Thanks." I'd not said that for praise, although his words made me feel good. "It's just odd," I confessed, using my fork to move a fatty chunk of steak through the garlic sauce that had run off the potatoes. I peeked at Oli. His gaze met mine. I saw nothing judgmental or accusatory in his eyes. He could have been really pissy about me and his best friend. I'd ghosted Jamie after sleeping with him and then I had bolted on an important research study that his bestie was running. Not exactly batting a thousand with either man, to be honest.

"Why odd?" He pushed another half a buttered bun through the juices on his plate. A woman's laugh carried over to us.

"I don't know." I shrugged. "I think maybe we shouldn't have had drunken sex that night."

"Do you regret it?"

"No, no, not at all! It was the best sex…" He cocked an eyebrow. "Well, you don't need to hear the graphic details. It was great, and I really wanted to be with him. I've been attracted to him for a while. But I have this past, and it's all tangled up with Jamie and his brain and Leon and his brain and me and my brain."

"That's a lot of brains," he commented dryly.

I snorted in amusement. "Yeah, a lot of brains. And mine is… mine is trying to sort itself."

"If I can ask, this Leon, is that the man you were seeing a few years ago? Big, strapping German fellow?"

"Yeah, that's him. He's incredibly smart and incredibly controlling. I'm not sure why he keeps trying to win me back because when he had me all he did was tell me how useless and stupid I was. Shit, okay, that wasn't supposed to come out over lunch. I'm sorry."

"Nope, don't be sorry." He placed a hand on my arm and gave it a fatherly squeeze. "It explains a lot. I'm so sorry that man was so cruel to you. He sounds as though he needs a good shoulder check into the boards. Several times. With intent to injure." That made me chuckle. "I don't want to push too far into your friendship with Jamie. What I will do is say this. Jamie would never knowingly berate you or strive to make himself feel like the bigger man just to feed a massive ego. He's far too kind."

"I know, I do, I just…" I blew out a breath that billowed my cheeks. "It's hard to trust again, you know? Every put-down Leon hurled at me is carved into my flesh, into my soul, and I'm trying to heal the wounds, but the scars are still tender."

"Sounds like you and Jamie both have some rotten exes. That's at least one thing you have in common. I wager if you two sat down and could keep your hands to yourselves for ten minutes, you'd discover you have more in common than you think. My friend may be incredibly smart but he's also incredibly loving. Not many people would uproot their lives to come live with a buddy and his two kids. He's just that special of a man." He shook his head. "I'm also incredibly biased, so move at your own speed. Just know that Jamie would do anything to clear up this misunderstanding."

I gave him a nod. We left that topic to wither for now, talking instead about hockey, and his kids. Nothing heavy. We'd already done the dense talk, and it had left me feeling lighter, and with some clarity of action.

It took me a few hours to work up the nerve to send out a simple text. With the memory of Jamie's hot skin next to mine in a rumpled bed, I dictated a message, had the phone read it over for mistakes, found five—*OMG, focus Craig* —fixed it, and then sent it out into the world. Right to Jamie's phone.

Hey, sorry about the study incident. Totes on me. If you'd like to have me back, I'd like to try again. ~ Craig

Chapter Nine

Jamie

THE SCENT OF STEW FROM THE SLOW COOKER FILLED THE kitchen, and at the kitchen table, the atmosphere bustled with the paper-and-pen-scratching, ultra concentration of homework time. Scarlett was showing off a colorful poster she'd crafted for a litter-picking event, vibrant and meticulously detailed, catching Oli's attention the moment he walked past with a mug of coffee for him and an extra one for me. He hadn't been home long but showered and dressed in his usual Storm T-shirt and shorts, he would always come and sit for homework time if he could.

"We all have homework!" Scarlett declared proudly, waving her poster at her dad.

Oli made all the right noises of approval. "Looks fantastic, Scarlett!" he praised, then leaned over to inspect Daisy's spelling homework, his expression switching seamlessly to encouragement. "Can you spell that?" he asked her, as Daisy glanced up at him and wrinkled her nose.

"Because. B-E-C-A-U-S-E. Because."

"That's amazing; I can barely spell that," Oli said and ruffled her hair.

While the girls were absorbed with their tasks, I spent any moment I wasn't needed shuffling papers and peering at an iPad, scribbling notes intermittently, deeply engrossed in a different kind of study.

"What homework do you have? Doesn't look like math," Oli asked, glancing over my shoulder with a curious frown.

"It's maths," I corrected automatically, without looking up from the screen.

"But it's not math, is it?" Oli pointed at the array of articles and notes spread out before me.

"No, I meant, maths is short for…" I glanced up and saw Oli trying not to snicker at me. Wanker. I snapped out of my research daze, realizing I hadn't explained my sudden shift in focus. "I'm researching dyslexia," I confessed, feeling weary.

"For working with Craig, right?" Oli probed gently but with a knowing tone.

I groaned, rubbing the back of my neck. "Does everyone except me know about his dyslexia?"

"Wait, you didn't know?"

I muttered no, and then sighed heavily. "No, I didn't, and so I put him in a shit situation, and now I feel guilty and stupid. I just launched into research without due diligence, which means I have to rethink with respect to accessibility, which I should have done from the start, and which I always do, but no, I was too caught up in what Sean did to me, and so desperate to get on with the project that I never even thought about the people I was researching with and…" Everything had fallen out of me in one long rush, and I exhaled noisily. "I fu—messed up," I added.

"I'm sure you didn't."

I slid my phone over to Oli and showed him the message from Craig.

Oli read it out loud. "Hey, sorry about the study incident. Totes on me. If you'd like to have me back, I'd like to try again."

"See? Now he's blaming himself, and it was I who didn't think, and I need to tell him that it wasn't on him, but he'll just think I'm being British and apologizing, when I crossed every academic line by not only making a mess in the study, but also one here." I gestured above our head at the bedrooms.

Oli chuckled, pulling out a chair to sit beside me. "I should have mentioned it."

"I should have interviewed my participants properly."

"You didn't know."

"But you did."

"Craig volunteers for the Dyslexia Foundation, works with kids, raises money for the charity. Did a half marathon last year for them and raised a hell of a lot of money. It's literally the first thing he mentions in any interview. I thought you knew."

I sighed, a flush of embarrassment warming my cheeks. "I didn't know. I didn't… research him much past…" I trailed off, aware of how it would sound admitting my initial interest in including Craig in the study had not been purely academic.

Oli gave me a sympathetic look, understanding more

than I wished he would. "It's all right, Jamie. Maybe it's a good thing. You're learning more about him now, right? It's not just about the study anymore."

"Yeah," I admitted, feeling a mix of frustration and gratitude. "It's definitely more than just the study now." I took a deep breath, resolving to approach my research—and my budding relationship with Craig—with a new perspective, one that acknowledged his strengths and challenges alike, and didn't mess up.

"Uncle Jamie, can I spell favorite for you?"

I blinked at Daisy, switching back to nanny/uncle instantly. "Of course." I listened as she spelled it out, exchanging a smile with Oli at the missing U, and then praised her success. Daisy and Scarlett might not be my nieces by blood, but they were family in my heart, and everything they did made me feel light.

"Is this the right purple?" Scarlett asked me, but Oli got there first.

When they were done choosing the right pen, he turned his gaze back on me as I sipped my coffee and stared at my iPad. "You should message him back."

"And say what?"

"I'm guessing you already apologized to him?"

"Of course, the minute it happened."

"So how about skipping your insane need to apologize for apologizing about the apology, and instead, ask to talk to him about his needs, and what you want from this project with him, and also how you'd like to take him on a date because he's not been playing at his best and I can only think what you're telling me has something to do with it."

I blanched at how inappropriate that sounded, also that I'd messed with his hockey mojo. "I'll suggest a meeting."

Oli smacked the back of my head, and Scarlett snickered. "I said a date! How about asking him for a coffee? Just a chat, not a full-blown meeting with minutes, but an honest-to-goodness chat."

I considered Oli's words. "It would be good to iron out the parameters of the study."

"Just coffee! Not science."

He picked up my phone and damn him, even though it had timed out, he knew me well enough to know my code was the girls' birthdays. Before I could stop him, he was tapping away at the screen, holding me back with his hockey body, and I heard the *whoosh* of a message being sent.

"What did you do!" I asked as he passed me the phone with his smug I-know-everything expression.

And I stared down at the horror that was the message he'd sent.

"How about a coffee date? Are you free this evening?" I blinked and read it again. "Tonight? He won't be available on short notice to—"

An incoming message interrupted my speech, and I handed the phone wordlessly to Oli, who grinned down at the message.

Sure, I know some places. I'll pick you up at seven, and if you haven't eaten, we can do Italian food. Or just coffee if you have.

"Girls?" Oli leaned towards Scarlett and Daisy. "Uncle Jamie has a date; you want to dress him up?"

The girls squealed so loud my eardrums hurt. Oli grinned.

And me?

I about died on the spot.

CRAIG'S SUV PULLED UP RIGHT AT SEVEN. IT WAS A couple of years old and nothing as flashy as I expected from a probably-millionaire hockey player with no family to support. Hell, I didn't know what I was expecting—maybe some low-slung, flashy sports car—but the modest Hyundai was a surprise. I stood by the curb, acutely aware of Oli and the girls peering out from the living room window. Turning to wave at them, to let them know I could see they were watching, I then slid into the passenger seat.

"Hey," Craig said with a smile.

He was dressed simply, yet every choice accentuated the best of his athletic build. His dark pants, stretched over his muscular hockey thighs, paired with a shirt casually unbuttoned at the throat, offered a glimpse of skin I wanted to taste. As I buckled myself in, I couldn't help but feel slightly out of place in my carefully chosen outfit. My favorite waistcoat felt a bit too formal now, even though I had paired it with plain trousers and a pale blue shirt. The subtle elegance of the ensemble usually gave me a comforting sense of preparation, but next to Craig's effortless style, I wondered if I was overdressed.

"Is this too much?" I gestured at myself.

"No."

Well, that was a simple answer, but it didn't alleviate my worrying. Then, there was no more time for questions as we pulled away from the curb, the car humming softly as Craig navigated the quiet evening streets. The silence wasn't uncomfortable, but my mind raced with all the words I wasn't saying. If he wasn't careful, I would end up talking about the weather just to fill the silence.

As if sensing my self-conscious musings, Craig glanced over with a small, knowing smile. "Can I say what I really think?" he asked, his voice smooth, almost cautious but he sounded as if he wanted me to answer. What was he going to say about what? What did he think?

"Okay," I responded, my voice tinged with a mix of curiosity and apprehension.

He kept his eyes on the road, but I saw his smile broaden. "I think you look perfect."

The words washed over me with a mix of relief and a flutter of something deeper, something that warmed me more than any compliment had in a long time.

"Thanks," I managed to say, my voice steady but my heart beating a little faster than usual. "You look perfect, too."

He smiled briefly, his attention fully on the road as he continued to drive. The ease between us grew, settling into the spaces of the car, and I found myself looking forward to not only dinner but to whatever we called this, a meeting, or a date, or whatever.

"Have you eaten?" Craig asked, his voice casual.

"No, not yet."

"There's a Thai place nearby, or I know a great Italian spot if you'd prefer?"

"Whatever you want."

"I want you to decide."

Oh, Jesus, that wasn't one of my good points. *Don't overthink this.* "Thai sounds good," I decided.

"Good choice. It's not far, just about ten minutes," Craig informed me, Lady Gaga humming softly through the stereo. The drive was quick, filled with trivial chat about the unusually hot weather and brief mentions of sports, topics that were safe but barely skimmed the surface of what was really on my mind.

Soon, we arrived at the Thai restaurant. Like his car, it wasn't flashy. We were greeted warmly and led to a private table at the back, each space designed to give diners a sense of privacy. As we settled in, I opened the menu, scanning the options, but then a thought struck me—how could Craig read the menu? I glanced up and the menu was closed in front of him, and I don't know what I was expecting, but my research had revealed special overlays that sometimes helped. Should I offer to read it out?

Craig seemed to notice my gaze, and my pause. "I've got my ways of dealing with everything," he said with a slight smile, "watch and learn." The waitress approached, and Craig was quick to order. "I'll have whatever the chef recommends today, and some mixed starters. No allergies," he said confidently, then asked for water.

I closed my menu, feeling slightly more at ease. "I'll have the same," I said to the waitress, "but could I get a beer with mine?"

Craig chuckled, a sparkle of humor in his eyes. "Just make sure it's not one of those warm beers, huh? Don't want Jamie here to feel too much at home."

The teasing comment eased the tension I hadn't realized I was feeling, particularly when I wasn't sure the waitress totally understood the joke. She smiled though, then walked away. When it was just the two of us, I found myself relaxing into the chair, the initial awkwardness dissipating.

As we settled into the quiet corner of the restaurant, the ambiance softened around us, filled with the gentle clatter of dishes and distant conversations. It was the right moment for more personal revelations, and I knew I needed to address the discomfort lingering between us since that meeting. Now was a good time to apologize but get him to see I'd learned from my mistake.

"Your message to me sounded as if you were apologizing."

"I was."

"It wasn't on you." He seemed as if he wanted to talk so I rushed ahead. "I want to apologize for putting you on the spot."

"I appreciate that," he responded, his voice measured but warm. "But—"

"No, it wasn't on you. I just get overexcited, and some things have happened in my research recently, so I just barreled ahead, and I didn't take the time to consider the people aiding my research. I mean you made me think, and it was a shit thing to do to you, and I've been considering a lot about accessibility in my research—realizing not all accessibility issues are obvious. I promise to be more considerate about such things in the future."

I sat back in my chair, a knot loosening in my chest

where I'd managed to get the whole thing out without going bright red.

Craig nodded, his expression softening. "Thanks for saying that. But it's my turn to explain and... hell, I'm sorry for overreacting," he said, a hint of vulnerability flashing across his face. "It's just that my ex made me feel inadequate, pointed out when I embarrassed him, which happened a lot according to him."

"What a wanker," I snapped in Craig's defense.

Craig snorted a laugh. "Say that again."

"What?"

"About my ex."

I huffed. "Wanker."

He reached for my hand. "Your accent is so sexy. Am I allowed to say that?"

Great, and now I was red, probably like a tomato.

"Yeah, as long as you don't call me cute in a Hugh Grant *Four Weddings* kind of way."

He bit his lip. "But you are cute. Sexy-cute. And your hair is soft and..." He leaned in a little. "I want to bury my hands in it and kiss you again."

I let out a sound that was a combination of a meep and a groan. "I want you to do that."

He lowered his voice. "The sex we had was insanely hot, right?"

I nodded. *Use my words.* "Yeah. Hot." *Where were my words? WORDS!*

"Can I ask you a question?" He sat back in his seat, and I unconsciously lifted my arse from the seat as if I was going to follow him. I nodded and sat myself back down. "Is this a date?"

Fuck. Was this a trick question? "Do you want it to be?" I hedged.

"Yes."

"Then yes, it is. I want it to be."

He dipped his gaze for a moment. "But can we take it really slow?"

I was torn between saying I wanted him to fuck me over the table and also saying I could move as slow as a glacier if that was what he wanted.

"Yeah," I said, as the waitress came over with drinks and tiny plates of starters. "We can do slow."

No one has ever died of blue balls. Right?

Chapter Ten

Craig

I WAS PRETTY SURE I WAS GOING TO DIE OF BLUE BALLS.

Dating Jamie was amazing. Going slow? Meh, not as incredible as I'd envisioned it to be, but it was helping us learn about each other. Which was why, two weeks into our officially slow dating regime, I was jerking off more than I had when I'd been fourteen. Which was a lot.

I wondered if I should contact my financial advisor and have him drop some cash into lube and tissue stock. Given how much of both items I was using, the stock had to be rising steadily. We'd barely even kissed the four times we'd been out. A peck on the cheek and a soft goodbye was all I'd gotten. Which was fine. Good. It was good. The only downside was that I knew what he tasted like, and I yearned for more. And not just taste. I wanted to touch him, smell him, hear him, see him moving on my dick. If I'd never experienced being with him—in him—I wouldn't have known what I was missing. Being able to replay that night of passion made denying myself much more painful. Like giving up cheesy doodles for Lent. I knew the little cheese curls were delicious, and so that long stint of denying myself was twice as rough compared to if I'd not known the glory that were Cheetos.

"Fuck," I groaned then shoved the heel of my hand into the raging boner in my shorts.

Sitting outside the movie theater in my SUV waiting for Jamie to show up for date five, I was not happy with the erection popping to life down yonder. "Chill out." I inhaled and exhaled. My dick didn't follow suit. "Stupid thing." I gave it another shove then tried to bring up some mental images of something disgusting. The only thing I could envision was a shudder-worthy memory of my great Aunt Tippie modeling the bikini she'd worn to catch Uncle Roger's eye back in 1968.

A sharp rap on the window jarred me out of the horrors of Tippie in that crocheted bikini. I blinked at Jamie smiling at me through my window. I smiled back, peeked down at my now flaccid prick, and then exited my SUV.

"You looked a thousand miles away," Jamie said as he leaned in to kiss my cheek. I really wanted to turn my head to meet his lips, but I bussed him back. All friendly and not Grabby McGrabby Hands the way I wanted to.

"Reliving childhood trauma," I confessed as I held out my hand. He threaded his fingers through mine as he glanced at me with mild confusion. The night was a sticky one, rain was being predicted for the area. Sorely needed rain as the woods were dry as tissue paper. Everyone in this state lived in a heightened awareness of how easy a wildfire started. And those nimrods who didn't heed the fire conditions needed a sharp kick in the balls. "Nothing too severe, just an old lady in a skimpy swimsuit."

"Gods, that's quite the trauma." A rolling rumble of thunder moved over the city, and we both glanced skyward. "We'd best get into the theater. I don't want to get my new silk shirt and coat wet."

He did look fantastic. Always so well-dressed and perfectly groomed. Some nights I felt like a schlub next to him. People were probably wondering what this stunningly smart and sexy man was doing with a puck-pushing jock. I wondered that myself almost every day. Then I thanked my lucky stars that Jamie seemed to be into big jocks.

We'd just entered the lobby of a retro theater, recently redone to resemble an old movie palace, when the first raindrops began to fall.

"Just in time," Jamie noted, then tried to offer me money for his ticket. I paid before he could argue too vehemently. "I'm buying the snacks."

"Works for me." I'd not had time to eat since lunch. I'd spent the afternoon at a car dealership, the same one I bought my new car from, shooting a commercial. Then I'd raced to a dyslexia support group over in Glendale where I'd sat with parents, educators, and caregivers of kids with learning disabilities. We'd discussed my journey, the ups and downs of parenting dyslexic kids, and the recent bill giving several million dollars to local schools to enhance their early intervention for children with learning disabilities programs. I'd been scheduled for an hour, but I was there for three with only some terrible coffee to fill my belly.

Ten minutes later, we headed to the theater with our arms loaded. Well, *my* arms were loaded, Jamie had a diet soda and some gummy bears.

"That might be the largest accumulation of junk food I have ever seen." He chuckled as we found our seats in the back row—far left—and settled in.

"Crispin, the new team dietician, would birth a water buffalo if he saw this." I snickered, placing my jumbo popcorn with extra butter on the thigh closest to Jamie so he could dip into the tub if he so desired. I tore into the first of five candy bars then washed it down with a few sips of my lemon-lime soda.

"So, since we have time to kill, let's pick up our getting-to-know-you game from the last date," he suggested, then popped a red bear into his mouth. I nodded with a mouth full of nougat and caramel. The crash from all of this sugar was going to be epic. "I'll go first. What was the name of your first pet?"

"Mm, easy. Her name was Piggles. She was the meanest Guinea pig ever to walk the earth. My sister lived in abject fear of Piggles. To this day she's leery of anything smaller than a cat."

Jamie laughed softly before eating a grape bear. He was so meticulous. One bear at a time, chew politely, swallow, and then pick another bear. I'd probably dump half the box into my pie hole at once. I loved that about him.

"My turn." I washed down candy bar three with more soda. "Do British people get schooling in being fussy?"

"'Fussy'?" He sat up in a huff, touched his chest, and gave me an icy look. "I am *not* fussy."

"You eat one bear at a time," I pointed out. He pursed his lips. "And you fold and iron your hankies. Your hair is always on point, and your trousers always have a crease pressed into them. Oh, and you dust off my car seat with that crisp handkerchief before you sit in it. Shall we even mention the waistcoats, which I think are amazing and super-hot? Ergo and to whit, you are an adorable fussbudget."

"I'm not roasting you like a chicken on a spit because you said I was adorable." I winked at him and got a playful eye roll in return. "The reason I dust off your car seat is because they generally have a fine coating of orange Wotsits dust."

"Okay, yeah, that's totally fair, they do."

He waggled a brow, just a bit, and then stole some popcorn from the bucket.

"I will say that your using ergo and to whit has my dick a little hard."

I nearly choked on my bite of candy bar number four. The lights lowered, and then they flickered several times before going off. A moment or two passed with no preview trailers, the only lights in the theater from cellphones and emergency exit signs over the doors.

"Must be the power is out," Jamie said in the dark.

"Do you want to leave or wait and see if it comes back on?" I asked as several people rose and made their way to the lobby. The film was an older one, a classic noir black and white from the forties that Jamie and I both loved. That was one thing we'd discovered about each other now we were talking and not rutting like wild stags. We both love the old detective flicks. Tonight, it was supposed to be *The Maltese Falcon* so, as you'd expect, the ticket holders were few and far between.

"I'm not in a rush to dash out into a deluge. Let's just see what happens."

So, we sat, talked, and waited with only the subtle light from the exit signs. "Tell me about your first crush," he prompted, then plucked one popped kernel from the tub. He was such a fussy, tidy, sexy man.

"I was four, and I told my father I was going to marry this boy called Julian." I wiped my buttery fingers on a wad of sticky napkins shoved between my thighs. "My parents weren't surprised. I don't recall saying much about Julian other than he had red hair and threw sand at Oscar the Biter."

"Oh dear, a biter. Nothing worse," Jamie replied with humor, then plucked another bite of popcorn from the tub. "Unless you're talking about vampires, then a neck nibble is just fine. What do you think of the new vampire series?"

"Oh, the one with the big guy and the witches, and—"

"Yeah."

"Jeez, I think I'd be happy to be bitten by any of the men on that show," I replied honestly before taking the final bite of candy bar five, a peanut and caramel delight. "Now, tell me about your first crush."

"Mm, well, her name was Penelope. I was about five or so, and she lived next to us. I think it was more a case of my mum and her mum pushing us together as parents like to do. As if, at five, you want or even care about having a girlfriend or boyfriend. Quite silly all of it, and then there's the assumption that a boy will automatically gravitate to a female. Yes, the chances are higher, but I do think that we need to stop pushing a heteronormative agenda on our children. Were your parents upset that you decided on young Julian as a future spouse?"

"Not really. Dad was incredibly accepting of the queer community. He has a cousin who's a lesbian. And my mom tells me that she suspected I was queer way before Julian entered my life. Seems I lived for *RuPaul's Drag Race*."

"I do love drag queens. Did you ever paint your face?"

"All the time. Mom has pictures."

"Mm, interesting. Would you ever consider a dash of eyeliner or some lipstick now?"

I paused in my chewing. He was quite intent on my reply. "If it was something to titillate a special lover, I might be willing to doll up a bit. How do you feel about men in corsets and stockings?"

"I think I look rather sexy in them."

I choked on a kernel. He thumped my back. "We'd best get back on track. Where was I? Oh yes, Penelope. Our garden fences were slotted, and she would pass me biscuits through the slots and ask for a kiss in exchange."

"Did she butter them?"

"The kisses?"

"What? I… no, the biscuits. They're dry if you don't have some butter or jelly on them."

"No, oh gods, you Americans. A cookie. She passed me a cookie through the slot."

"Oh, a cookie." He reached over the tub to rub his fingers on the napkins held between my thighs. The back of his fingers slid over my leg. It was like grabbing hold of an electric fence if that fence was hooked on a direct line to your balls. One soft touch. Massive jolt of lust. I gasped and jerked, spilling some popcorn on the floor. "Damn, ticklish. Sorry. Cookies, right, cookies for kisses."

Jamie sat there like a statue, his gaze locked on me as I stuttered on about trading cookies for kisses.

"We could have been doing that. Penelope was quite clever now that I think on it," he said, his hand settling on my thigh.

"I don't have any cookies," I blurted then winced at my dumb reply. It was hard to think with all my blood now pooled in my groin. My dick throbbed. If the tub had been a few inches to the right, my cock would have knocked it to the floor.

"Popcorn for kisses."

"Oh, yeah, popcorn for kisses. We should have been. That Penelope was quite the budding businesswoman. How many cookies did you swap?"

"About a dozen. Got a terrible stomach ache and a lecture about kissing people through the garden fence." He moved his hand, thank God, and lifted a single kernel from the tub, his fingers glistening in the dim light. I watched, spellbound, as he placed it on his tongue and then pulled it into his mouth. The way he chewed was hot. "Now, since I got a treat, you get a kiss."

"Okay," I said brilliantly.

Words were too hard to untangle right now. On good days—with no sensual Brit leaning over an armrest with a cup of soda resting in it—my head had fits with vocabulary. With his lips pressed to mine, there was no way I was cooking up anything witty to say. Which was totally fine with me. I had better things to do with my tongue than articulate. It was put to much better use sliding between his buttery, salty, plush lips. I placed my hand on the back of his neck, massaging the nape, as his tongue met and then knotted with mine. The kiss was wet, sloppy, and hot. He made these delightful little sounds of pleasure that took me right back to our night of lust and how bossy of a bottom he had been. I wanted to peel him out of his pretty clothes, throw his glasses aside, and plow his ass like a newly worked alfalfa field.

An unexpected burst of sound and light filled the theater. We parted guiltily, both of us panting softly. The film choked a few times, skipping right to the scene of San Francisco then a close-up of a window overlooking the city, *SPADE AND ARCHER* painted on the glass.

"Much as I love Bogart I'd rather look at your face," I whispered my confession. He reached up to stroke my cheek. A few people returned and took their seats.

"We'll return to kissing later," he confided before letting his head come to rest on my shoulder.

Later was good. Not as good as right now but given we had to share the musty theater with five other people I'd have to settle for later. I sat back to drink in Sam Spade rolling a smoke as Effie informed him about a knockout dame in the outer office.

The next hour and forty minutes raced by. Even though I knew the movie inside and out, it never lost its appeal to me, and to Jamie, it seemed, as he was smiling throughout the screening. When Sam walked off holding the Falcon after uttering that famous line about the stuff that dreams are made of, the seven of us in the theater applauded loudly. The lights slowly rose in brightness.

"How great is that movie?" I asked Jamie as we gathered up our trash and headed for the lobby. "I can watch that a thousand times."

"Same here. Oh hell." He sighed while I dumped the empty tub filled with candy wrappers into a large garbage can beside the snack shop. "It's still raining."

I turned to look out of the glass doors. The dark streets were puddled, the steady pitter-patter of rain hitting the puddles and making them dance.

"We can make a dash for it," I offered as the other moviegoers ran out into the deluge with coats or arms over their heads.

"Right. Let's do that then." He peeled off his waistcoat, balled it tightly, and then tucked it under his arm like a football. "On the count of three. One, two—"

I bolted out of the door on two. I heard Jamie call me a wanker as I ran outside, the rain soaking me in no time. Jamie splashed after me, catching up when I skidded to a halt to wrap him in my arms.

"Oof! What the bloody hell are you doing?" He laughed out loud, his glasses dotted with rain, his hair flat to his head.

"We're doing the more kissing thing now," I said then captured his mouth. He sighed into the kiss, opening for me, his free hand clutching at my sodden shirt. We stood there under a flickering streetlight making out as if it were a clear night. We only broke apart when a low rumble of thunder rolled over us. I drew back, just an inch, and cupped his wet cheek. "I think we should do lots more dating and kissing."

"I so agree. Shall we stroll to the cars?"

"Yes." He took my arm, and we sashayed to our rides, sniggering madly, as the heavens rained down. Anyone passing by may have heard us humming "Singing in the Rain" amid the snorts and giggles of two men falling deeply into feelings for each other.

Chapter Eleven

Jamie

HOW IS THIS MY LIFE?

I was fervently defending the merits of Marmite, trying to convince Jackson of its legendary status back in Britain. "You haven't lived until you've eaten Marmite on toast," I insisted, spreading a generous layer on a piece of toast to demonstrate.

Jackson made a face that clearly showed his skepticism. "That stuff looks like tar!" he exclaimed, backing away with exaggerated horror. Then, with a playful shout toward the living room where Oliver was flipping lazily through a sports magazine, he yelled, "Oli, your best friend is trying to kill me with this... this motor oil on toast!"

Oliver laughed from the other room, not bothering to look up. "Just eat it, Jack! It's an acquired taste!"

"You couldn't pay me enough to even sniff it, let alone eat it," he muttered.

Along with my Yorkshire tea and my supply of custard creams, Marmite was one of the other things I'd found online to order in, and after Oli suggested I have a cupboard in the kitchen for my Brit-stuff, as he called it, I now had five jars of Marmite in stock, three packages of biscuits, and over a thousand tea bags.

Just in case.

"It stinks," Jackson said with a theatrical sniff.

"Don't you have donuts to buy and bad guys to arrest, Columbo?" I deadpanned.

He rolled his eyes. "Don't stereotype me, *Hugh*."

"Do I need to break this up?" Oli asked, and bumped Jackson off his stool.

"You need to take that black stuff away from here," Jackson said with an exaggerated shudder. "Like far, *far* away."

"Says the man who can't taste the hot dog for the mustard," I hit back, and couldn't help the smile. Jackson was growing on me—he was good for Oli, and as to Oli and the girls? Well, Oli was besotted, and the girls loved Jackson. Although they still came to me first if they needed something.

Take that Columbo—Brit 1, Cop 0.

"Isn't your meeting at ten?" Oli asked, glancing up at the clock, and the kitchen banter over my choice of breakfast was interrupted by my sudden realization of the time.

"Damn, I'm late to the rink," I muttered, checking my watch frantically as if it was going to say something different. I needed to brush my teeth, check my notes, and god knows what else before I could even leave the house.

An amused smirk played on Jackson's lips. "Why the

rush, Jamie? Got a hot date or something at the rink?" he teased.

"It's not a date. I need to gather data today," I shot back.

Jackson, who was still eyeing the Marmite toast suspiciously, chuckled. "Is that what the cool kids are calling it these days?" His teasing only added to the light-hearted conspiracy brewing against my serious intentions. I might be dating Craig, hell we might have had three dates since the cinema that included a serious amount of kissing, but I wasn't at the feeling-okay-being-teased stage yet.

I tipped my chin. "Yes, I *am* dating Craig, but *no*, today is *not* a date."

"He's only teasing." Oli elbowed Jackson who snorted a laugh. "We leave in five."

Ignoring Jackson's laughter, I hurried upstairs, did what I needed, grabbed my notes, and met Oli at the door, ready to dart out, but not before hearing Jackson's comment in his best approximation of a Hugh Grant accent. "Take your 'data gathering' seriously, mate!"

"Jackson is an arsehole," I muttered to Oli as I belted in.

"Sarcasm is his love language." Oli grinned at me and waited for the gates to open before heading downtown to the Storm practice arena. "There was something..." He stopped as the lights changed, and he merged into the traffic.

"Something what?" I prompted.

"Never mind," he said, his concentration on driving.

I sighed. "If you have something to say about me and Craig then stop, I know you never liked Sean, and you were right, but you're not my dad and I lo—I like Craig. Okay?"

Oli shot me a sharp look at my near slip. "That wasn't what I was going to say."

I tipped my chin. "No?"

"No, I was going to… wait a minute…" He indicated to turn into the rink parking, flashed his security pass, and pulled up in the first space he found, which was easy given there were only a couple of other cars parked there, one of which was Craig's. "I'm thinking of asking Jackson to marry me," he blurted.

I spun in my seat to face him. "You're doing what?" I asked to give me a moment to think about how to react. Jackson was a teasing, annoying asshole, but he was also a good guy, loved Oli and the girls, and hell, I liked him as well. Even if he did keep stealing my Custard Creams, and probably secretly loved Marmite.

Or not.

"You think it's a bad idea?" Oli asked, as if my opinion mattered.

"God no, I was just shocked, that's all. It was inevitable it would happen," I said.

"Really?"

"He loves you, you love him, I just… is he the settling down kind of person?"

Oli grinned. "Yeah, he is."

"He's moved in," I said.

"He has."

"The girls love him."

"They do."

"And you love him."

"I do."

I pressed a hand to his arm. "So why are you only *thinking* of asking him to marry you?"

He blinked at me, and it was as if any doubt he might be having that Jackson wasn't his forever slipped away. "I'm not," he said and sat back in his seat. "I'm *not* thinking. I *am* going to ask him."

"Congratulations, bestie." I tugged my best friend into an awkward sideways hug. "You found your man, you keep him."

"And if he says yes…"

"*When* he says yes."

"You'll be my best man?"

Emotion choked me. I'd seen so much of his grief after Melissa died, of the way he was with the girls, how he'd finally found a new love, and I was so happy for him.

"Of course I will."

He gripped my arm and grinned. "One day soon, I'm gonna ask Jackson to marry me."

"And I'll babysit when you do it."

"You won't need to. I have this idea…"

"What idea?"

"Never mind." He rested his forehead on mine. "You're a good friend, Jameson Hennessy." Then he sat back and gestured for me to get out. "Now, go data collect."

I grinned at him, happy with the world, and now I was going into *data collect* with Craig. This was a good morning.

THIS WAS SO *NOT* A GOOD MORNING.

"I don't understand why you're making me bloody skate, for god's sake," I said for the millionth time. And yes, I was exaggerating, but I'm a doctor of mathematics, so sue me. For some ungodly reason, Craig had extra skates with him, and this wasn't just going to be me documenting him when he was determined to get me out on the ice.

"So, you can feel what it's like from a practical point of view," he said again.

Despite my better judgment, I was letting this happen and right now he was crouched in front of me, balanced on his skates, peering up at me from under his messy, flicky fringe, or bangs as they called them here, and no, I had no idea why. He was so beautiful down there, smiling at me as if he were giving me the world when actually he was giving me a pair of used skates and forcing me onto the ice upon which I would likely die.

As we approached the rink, all the injury statistics I had read up on came rushing back to me. "You know, the likelihood of injury on public ice rinks is statistically high for a first-time skater," I told him, hoping maybe this last fact could get me out of having to skate.

Craig just chuckled and handed me a pair of skates. "Well... one, this isn't a public rink. It's just us, and two, I'm right here with you."

Strapping on the skates had felt like gearing up for a dangerous mission, and neither of us was padded up like Craig was in a game. When I stepped onto the ice, my movements were awkward, reminiscent of a newborn deer's first steps. Craig stayed close, and I swear I was cutting off the circulation in his fingers by how tightly I gripped his hands.

"Just keep your knees bent and your weight forward a bit," he instructed, skating backward with ease in front of me.

I grimaced, attempting to mimic his posture while recounting another fact to distract myself from abject fear. "I read about this kid who lost a finger because someone skated over his hand."

"Jamie…"

"Look I know it's pretty rare, but you can see why I'm not thrilled about this."

Craig smiled at me. "You're safe with me, and no one's going to skate over your hands."

"If I fall—"

"You won't fall."

We took slow laps around the rink, Craig leading and occasionally pulling me along when I froze. Each time I swayed dangerously, his grip would tighten, steadying me.

"There you go, you're getting it," he encouraged, as we completed another shaky circuit.

I managed a weak smile, still tense but no longer terrified. "I'm really only doing this because I trust you, you know." Despite my anxiety and the chilling tales of ice rink mishaps, Craig's confidence and close presence made the experience bearable, and eventually, even a little enjoyable.

He chatted away, and I was caught up in his words as we moved on to his time playing college hockey, and how it was hard to fit in with studying.

"You know," Craig began, his voice reflective as he

tugged me in a slow spiral, "college was a real struggle for me at first. With dyslexia, everything just took twice as long, and the words… they just danced around the page."

That lined up with the research I'd done, and I couldn't imagine how hard it had been for him. I shifted my balance, and he corrected it—kept me upright.

"I can only imagine how tough that was. You always seem so together about everything."

He chuckled, a low, rueful sound. "Yeah, well, it wasn't always like that. I had to work my ass off just to keep up. Ended up having to get a personal tutor."

I couldn't resist a tease. "Oh, I've seen that porno. The needy student and the seductive nerd."

Craig laughed. "*Imogen* Mulroney was far from being my type, trust me. Plus, she was more like a drill sergeant than anything you'd find in those films. No nonsense, all business, no sex or spankings."

I laughed along with him, appreciating the ease with which he could joke about his challenges. It was one of the things I loved about him—his resilience and his ability to not take himself too seriously. I wish I had the skill to not take things über seriously at times.

"But y'know," he continued, becoming more somber, "having dyslexia made me feel as if I was always climbing uphill. Imogen helped a lot, though. She figured out ways to get through to me, techniques that I still use."

I wobbled slightly and he tugged me to the barrier where we stopped and hung for a while. "It's impressive, you know. Not everyone would have stuck it out."

Craig turned his hand to interlace his fingers with mine, giving a gentle squeeze. "Had to. I wasn't going to let it beat me. I wanted to prove that I could do it, despite the dyslexia." The pride in his voice was real.

I felt a surge of admiration for him. "And you did," I said. "You're one of the best people I know, Craig."

He smiled. A soft, thoughtful expression that made his eyes crinkle at the corners. "Thanks, Jamie. That means a lot. Now, back to skating."

"No, please, no."

He ignored me, tugging me back in circles and I tried my hardest to look cool. If cool is a grown man as useless as a baby on skates.

Craig laughed, keeping our pace slow and manageable. "You look so cute out here," he added, and I felt hot.

All over hot.

And so turned on by the capable way he was holding me up, and skating backward, and smiling all the time he was doing it. It would be so easy to fall in love with him, to imagine a life with him. But, when I did that, I wasn't focusing on my studies, and I needed to because Sean was out there riding the coattails of what he'd stolen from me. I needed to prove to him, and the mathematics community what I was capable of.

As if that errant flash of temper was enough to send my legs sideways and I ended up flat on my back, tit over arse, with Craig sprawled over me.

"I fell over," I said with a squeak of indignation.

He made no move to get off me, gently tangled his hand in my hair. "You look so good lying on the ice," he murmured, and I kind of melted there and then. Fuck statistics, I wanted a kiss.

Which led to another kiss, and another, until my back

was cold, and I was turned on, and Craig finally backed off and helped me stand.

"I need to collect data," I said, even as I reached for another kiss.

He chuckled and held me close for a moment. "Where do you want me."

"In bed," I blurted, and he tried not to laugh.

"I meant, here, today, spirals... y'know, out on the ice."

"Oh." I blinked at him. "That."

"Yep, that."

"I need to..."

I waved at the seats, and he guided me off the white stuff and helped me take off the skates and lace up my boots. Then I helped add an array of sensors to his jersey, his knees, and his ankles before he glided back out and waited.

"And?" he asked, a stick in his hand and a puck on the ice waiting. I glanced down at my notes and the empty spaces for stats and comments.

"Can you skate, but call on your figure skating days to..." I waved at the rink.

He grinned at me. "Skating I can do," he said.

As I watched Craig glide across the ice with precision, twisting and turning, I considered my theory of a connection between the natural spirals in Fibonacci sequences and the movements in ice hockey. The elegance of Craig's maneuvers from his figure skating past, the way he curved and swirled, almost traced mathematical patterns invisibly on the ice. My thesis was that the same principles dictating the growth patterns of sunflowers and seashells dictated the sweeping arcs of a gymnast, or a football player, or a hockey player. The way Craig pivoted and turned, each could be part of a larger, predictable pattern, perhaps even something that could be modeled mathematically. I took notes, watched my laptop collect data, and as he executed a particularly tight spiral, I pushed aside being turned on, to think logically. This was only the start of the data collection, requiring precise tracking of motions that were second nature and intuitive to players like Craig.

Lost in thought, I barely noticed Craig skating back toward me, a grin on his face, coming to a smooth stop that sent a small spray of ice crystals into the air.

"Was that enough? Or do you need more?"

I blinked at him, lost in equations forming and reforming as I considered variables like speed, angle of attack, and the physics of skates on ice.

"Huh?" I asked, and gazed at the screen where Craig's actions were tracked as strings of ones and zeroes.

"Do you need more?" he asked, and leaned on the barrier, his face flushed from the exercise.

The data was there, the skating was just day one of data collection, but there was only one thing I wanted to say. I shut my laptop and took the three steps to the barrier, leaning into him.

"Your numerical and geometric data is beautiful," I murmured. Oli had said Jackson's love language was sarcasm—well, mine was mathematics.

"My what now is what now?" Craig grinned.

I reached for him and cradled his face, and we kissed.

"You are beautiful."

Chapter Twelve

Craig

"Box!" Cam yelled as we wrapped up a fruitless power play against San Jose.

I spied the player leaving the penalty box as I streaked past the sin bin, the puck on my stick, and not a soul near me. The thunder of Cam taking out the player exiting the box with a check that rattled the boards and made the home fans cheer reached me as I zeroed in on the San Jose goalie who was tracking me like a hawk following a rabbit. He was a big Canadian, a lovely guy when you weren't on the ice. He was known to chop your legs if you got on his nerves. I was planning on getting on his nerves big time in a few seconds. He dropped low, closing his pads to block his five-hole. A player in bright teal appeared at my left, his stick swinging out in an attempt to lift mine. The stick hit my skate and bounced back at him. I moved to the left, shifted to take a backhand shot, and the puck flew cleanly over the tendie and into the net.

"Fuck yes!" I shouted as I sailed to the side to get hugs and pats from my line. That sweet little goal was my seventh in five games. Being in deep feelings with Jamie had not only improved my personal life but it had also done wonders for my game. Life was good. Everything was buttercups and butterflies.

We won that game handily, flogging San Jose with seven goals to their one. I'd pulled in a goal, two assists, five hits, four blocked shots, played over sixteen minutes, and ended with a great plus-minus of +2. The press were curious as to what had brought around my improvement. I told them I owed it all to prune juice. That got a laugh. I wasn't really the kind to broadcast my personal life, and so I played this new relationship with Jamie incredibly close to my vest. Not that I was ashamed. How could I be? He was smart and gorgeous and funny, even if he did add too many letters to his words. I wanted to take it slow and ease into the serious stuff after I was positive he was in this for the duration. I already knew he would never do me wrong as Leon had, but I was still scared. My sister assured me the fear would fade over time. I just needed to give Jamie a chance. Time to prove he was not a shitty Leon sort.

Deep down, I knew that. I had to convince my scarred and skittish heart.

Time. Claudia was hardly ever wrong about such things.

So, we kept dating, kissing, and getting to know each other while time slowly repaired my heart. Jamie was solid gold. I had told him that just last night, had whispered over his soft lips that his affection was gluing my heart back together.

"Like kintsugi." He chuckled as his fingers combed out my curls and then freed them.

"What's that?" I had asked, roughly nipping at his jaw as we rolled around on my sofa, his lean body pinned under me, his waistcoat lying over my coffee table.

"It's a form of Japanese pottery repair where the broken bits are rejoined using a special lacquer and then dusted with gold, silver, or platinum. I love how bouncy your hair is." I loved that imagery. My busted heart being pieced back together bit by bit, Jamie's gentleness being the glowing golden seams that would fix my shattered pieces. "It's a lovely philosophy. To embrace the imperfections."

I locked my elbows, rearing back enough to gaze down at him, wishing I could speak with the refinement he did.

"I really like you," fell out of my mouth.

His hot gaze grew warmer as his fingers, still in my hair, tugged me back down for a kiss that nearly set the couch cushions on fire. "We all have flaws, nicks, and chips, love. I'm just happy to be the gold dust being sprinkled over your healing heart."

He was way more than mere dust. He was a huge vein of precious metal, rich and shiny, filling my life with golden warmth.

The shouts of a happy team filing into the showers pulled me from the memories. Smiling at nothing in particular, I hustled around, eager to scour the sweat and stink of sixty minutes of hockey off my skin. Jamie and I were going to a local jazz club where some of his associates were having drinks. To say I was nervous would be an understatement. Jamie was introducing me to his brainiac friends. The niggling voice of self-doubt from the little boy who was teased unmercifully by the other kids for being slow for not being able to read always poked its head up when I was faced with this kind of situation. I swear Leon used to drag me to every damn big brain club gathering he could to ensure my ego stayed trodden down.

Tension radiated off me on the drive to pick up Jamie. I pushed it aside—no sense in filling his ear with my worries—and kissed him hello when he crawled into the front of my SUV looking as spiffy as ever.

"Do you ever not look like someone who waits on the king?" I asked as he buckled up.

"Better a footman than a barrister. Those powdered wigs are itchy," he replied with a smile that made me forget my name. "You look rather fetching. Congratulations on that game-winning goal! The girls and I were hooting like silly owls. Oliver has dropped hints that I need to keep kissing you so that you keep scoring goals."

"I like the sound of that," I replied earnestly.

"Then we'll have to ensure we keep kissing regularly for good goal health."

That made me laugh nervously.

"Are you sure everything is okay? You're sending off some weird vibes," Jamie asked.

I waved his worry off. There were a hundred jazz clubs peppered throughout LA and the surrounding counties. Leon was probably at one of the ritzier ones nestled tightly in Pacific Palisades or Bel Air where he lived. I was acting like a victim again. That had to stop.

By the time we arrived at Plum Pit Jazz Emporium on

South LaBrea Avenue, it was well past midnight. I was starved, as I always was after a game, and was praying this club had food. Thankfully, it had a full menu as well as a funky little quartet sitting on a stage backlit with plum-colored lights. The Plum Pit was two stories with a spiral staircase leading to the second floor. Servers in dark purple shirts hustled about delivering cocktails and platters of bar food. My stomach growled.

If it had been just us I would have tried to get Jamie upstairs for more privacy as people sort of knew my face. I wasn't LA-famous, but hockey folks knew me on the street. I loved the fans, I did, but when I was out I tended to be a little on the standoffish side now and again. Sometimes a person simply wants to be a person, unknown, left alone to enjoy his food or the music, or whatever was going on. I know it's all part of the pro-athlete thing. Play in a big market town, and you belong to the fans, or so many Storm backers felt.

Thankfully, the incredibly pushy fans were outnumbered a hundred to one by people who respected your privacy. Kids didn't count, obviously. Kids were always welcome no matter what I was doing.

Jamie found his people right off, a table of eight tucked behind an ivy-covered trellis in the corner, and he led me to them with his fingers meshed firmly with mine. Okay, this was a nice set-up. We were hidden from the front door and all those eyes. The stage was to our right, the bar and kitchen close at hand.

I smiled and nodded at the people waving at us, pleased as punch to be introduced to this group of scientists and math folks as his new boyfriend. It may have been a slip as we'd never discussed using the B-word for each other, but if it was a slip, then it was a slip I was fully behind. The names flew at me, and I tried to match the name with the face. Four men and three women, all seemingly polite and kind. We sat, ordered drinks, and asked for a menu for me. Then I lost the flow of conversation as Percy-with-the-freckles, a math professor of some sort, began talking about the general anti-science mentality overtaking the country, which led to everyone tossing things into the verbal hat. I had no clue. Socratic discussions about varying theorems and how to incorporate them into the college classroom left me sitting and sipping my ginger ale with a slice of lemon.

Jamie seemed to be enjoying himself. It must be hard to be such a learned man spending your days with two kids, a grumbly cop, and two hockey players. Not that we weren't smart, I mean Jackson, Oli, and I all had degrees. Granted they weren't in advanced mathematics or quantum math, but they were still degrees. Seeing Jamie getting so into the discussions, I settled back into my chair to enjoy the music. The beat was up-tempo. Brass horns filled the air.

I ordered a burger and fries from a passing server, then sat back to nurse my soda.

"I'm sorry," Jamie whispered in my ear a few minutes later when the band was taking a small break. "I've not tried to include you in any of the conversations."

"It's fine. I took you to Charlie's house last weekend, where we did nothing but sit on the floor, eat junk food, and play *NHL '24* for five hours. It's equalizing itself out."

He grinned, kissed me on the lips, and then moved his

chair a bit closer. "Well, I'm going to steer us into something less maths-oriented as soon as Rachel wraps up her bitch fest about teaching quantum mathematics to young adults who struggled with linear algebra yet somehow passed into college."

"That was me. The kid struggling with algebra."

"Jamie, are you dating a man who can't whisper enumerative algebraic combinatorics as pillow talk?" Freckled Percy asked, then sniggered into his Cosmopolitan.

Jamie ruffled like an angry rooster. I gave his thigh a pat under the table.

"I'm a hockey player, not a math professor, but so far, my pillow talk seems to be pleasing my man," I replied just as my burger and fries arrived.

"I just love it when you ask me to handle your big stick," Jamie purred.

Everyone at the table, aside from whom I suspected rather liked Jamie, roared. I pecked my boyfriend's scruffy cheek, then dove into my food. Things at the table quieted down after Percy left. He suddenly recalled he had papers to grade, and I was slowly brought into a lively discussion about the charity work the team and I were involved in.

The band returned as I ate my last seasoned French fry. I made a mental note to come here again—the food was so good. The music was nice too, not my general vibe but catchy.

"I'm going to go wash my hands," I told the table as I rose.

They were sticky with salty beef juices. Jamie smiled up at me. I moved through the crowd, sleepiness settling on my shoulders like a warm scarf now that my belly was full. I checked my phone as I waited outside the locked men's room door. It was now after two in the morning. I hid a wide yawn behind my phone. We'd have to go soon. I had morning skate at nine, and coming into practice dragging ass would get you chewed out. Coach expected his players to maintain good health habits, and one of the most important was proper sleep.

While I waited I sent Claudia a voice note. She'd be getting up in a few hours and would want to know how this meet-and-greet had gone. I'd vented to her earlier in the day about how anxious I was.

Hey C! So, the big brain squad has been super nice, aside from one of them who's crushing on Jamie, so he doesn't count. Goes to show not all big brains are big jerks. Give hugs and kisses to Bruno for me. Love ya. Talk later.

The band started playing a Kasami Washington song, *Askim,* one I had enjoyed a lot during my dark days with my ex. I'd always enjoyed the sound of a smooth saxophone and Kasami was one of the best in my humble opinion. Leon was a jazz enthusiast, a snob of the highest caliber, who made fun of anyone who wasn't as knowledgeable about the genre as he was.

The beautiful music was completely overshadowed by the remembrance of one terrible night being dragged through the mental mud for citing the incorrect album title at a small dinner party. Leon had latched onto my mistake like a steel trap, unwilling to stop berating my intelligence despite his stuffy friends trying to gently lead him onto another topic. Things got worse when they left.

He picked at me relentlessly, stripping me down to bloody bones before announcing that he wasn't sure he could even fuck a man as inferior as I was anymore. He'd locked me out of our bedroom—I'd made the mistake of moving in with him—for a week. When he deemed I'd learned my lesson he'd let me back into his bed.

"Fucker," I snarled softly as the memory picked at me like one does a torn hangnail.

The bathroom door opened. I glanced up from my shaking hand still holding my phone and into hazel eyes I knew far too well.

"Craig, imagine running into you here. Did you track me down here in order to admit your foolish mistake?" Leon asked, his short blond hair damp from where he had wet-combed it into submission.

I gaped at his beauty. He was stunning. Tall, broad-shouldered, lean-waisted, with a classic Germanic beauty. High cheekbones, sunny hair that disliked humidity and curled despite his best attempts to tame it. Seemed the only thing Leon Schmied couldn't get under his thumb was his hair. Everything and everyone else was firmly in his control. "You look surprised to find me here, yet you know I visit all the clubs."

His thick accent made me shudder. Was that shiver lust or disgust? It was hard to tell. I hated that I still found him so fucking pretty despite knowing what a horrid bully he was.

"I'm here with someone," I managed to cough out, the meat juices on my fingers completely forgotten.

"Oh?" He rose to his toes—he was a few inches taller

than me—and craned his head this way and that. "And what does this someone mean to you?"

"He's my boyfriend," I countered, using my shoulder to move him aside. He may have been taller, but I was a hockey player. I knew how to use a shoulder and an elbow.

"How droll." He stepped to the side to avoid the incoming check. Pity. It would have knocked him onto his ass. "As if anyone would wish to spend time with a dimwit."

I spun to face him; my hands fisted so tight I had to force myself to loosen the one gripping my cell phone.

"If I'm such a dimwit why are you begging me to come back to you?"

That got him on his heels but only for a moment. A litigator like Leon was never off-balance for long.

"That was an unfortunate word choice. I am sorry, seeing you here was so unexpected that it shocked me into speaking poorly."

His brown-green eyes were framed by lush brown lashes. The hair color was not God-given but was mixed by his stylist Olaf.

"You don't know how to speak any other way. I would like to end this discussion, so if you'd please move so I can use the bathroom?"

"Craig, don't be so callous. It is serendipitous that we met here. I've been yearning to—"

"Go yearn in your hand."

"You're being petulant again. It is not a good look on such a handsome face. You should smile more, Liebling."

"Seeing you makes me want to vomit not smile. Now move."

"I don't think you wish to be rude to me. Just remember whose name is on the pedigree papers."

"Bruno was a gift. You can't take back a gift."

"I wager a judge would think differently about that." He smiled at me, a demonic grin if ever I'd seen one. "You have no proof of your claims. I have the AKC papers citing me as his purchaser. That is all that I'd need."

"Possession is nine-tenths of the law," I fired back.

His left eyelid twitched, a sure sign I'd hit a nerve. "Do not *think* to argue legalities with me, Craig. Trust me, you will lose, and it will be a painful loss indeed. I suggest you ponder your choices well and try to make a sensible choice this time. This is why you require me to help you through your life, my pet."

The threat was subtle, nothing most guys would even pick up, but I heard it.

He drew in a slow breath that stretched the fabric of his Leon Boss dress shirt over his muscular chest. A woman wiggled past on her way to the lady's room, dark-lined eyes narrowing as she picked up the vibes between us.

"Here you are! Come on, baby, the rest of us are preparing to leave." She grabbed my arm and then tugged, sliding in to curl into my side as if we were together. Leon snorted. He knew full well I wasn't here with this pretty brunette with the big blue eyes, but he was smart enough to not act up in front of witnesses.

"It's been a pleasure running into you again," Leon purred, his sight locked on me as if the young woman wasn't even here. "I expect to hear from you within a week pertaining to my property. I've been more than patient with you about *their* return, but if I do not have them in my possession by Friday at five p.m., or have the appropriate financial restitution, I will press charges, and we *will* rehash our depressing relationship in court. What would come out would make Depp versus Heard look like a preschool sandbox spat. Wonder what the Storm would think of having all that hit the papers?"

He left us then, striding off to rejoin some pretentious group of friends. I watched him climb the circular stairs with a dull horror slowly starting to grow in my breast. If he sued me, then our sex lives, and much more, would be out there for public consumption. The Storm was very supportive of their queer players, but they wouldn't want me to be featured in a gay love story gone horribly wrong. I'd have to recount all the terrible things he'd said to me in front of a judge and jury and—

"You're trembling." I looked down at the little thing grasping my arm. What a brave woman she was. "I hope what I did was okay. I know that tone and the expression he was wearing. I've dated a few assholes like him. Was it cool that I stepped in?"

"Yeah, that was incredibly cool. Thank you. What's your name?"

"Lydia Lawrence. I know who you are. My boyfriend loves the Storm."

"This Sunday, bring your boyfriend to the game on me. I'll leave some tickets at Will Call for Lydia-the-brave Lawrence."

Her eyes rounded. "Oh wow, that would be great! Thank you so much, Craig." She rose to her toes to peck my cheek before releasing my arm. "Do you want me to escort you back to your table?"

"No, you go to powder your nose. I'll be fine."

She seemed unsure but then dashed off to the ladies' room. I shook off the encounter the best I could before returning to our table. Apparently, my powers of disguise were lacking. As soon as I sat down, Jamie glanced at me, and the soft smile he'd been wearing turned into a look of concern.

"You look upset. Did you not get into the men's room?"

"No, I never did get in. A huge pile of shit met me at the door." His brow wrinkled in confusion. "Can we go? I need to get out of here."

I stepped out into the clammy night, drew in a shuddery breath, and waited for Jamie to exit after settling our tab. What I would say to him I had no clue…

Chapter Thirteen

Jamie

THE NIGHT HAD A LAID-BACK VIBE, WITH JAZZ MUSIC weaving through the air, until Craig's mood took a sudden nosedive. When he came back to our table, I could tell something was off. His smile didn't quite reach his eyes, and he avoided looking directly at me as he said he wanted to leave. Had someone said something to upset him? Someone at this table? I couldn't recall anyone being rude, but sometimes the subtle nuances of communication went straight over my head. I settled our tab, still trying to figure out what might have turned his evening sour so quickly.

Had I done something wrong?

He said he'd run into a huge pile of shit, and his voice had been tinged with frustration and a hint of anger, uncomfortable. Whatever, I was happy to back him up if he needed to leave, and it was convenient enough to get us out without a fuss.

As I stepped out into the night, the cool air felt unusually sharp, cutting through the humidity that had settled over the city. The streets were dimly lit, with an occasional street lamp casting long shadows on the pavement. The usual buzz of the city felt subdued, almost like Craig's mood when I found him standing a few feet away from the jazz club's doorway, taking deep, shaky breaths. The evening had turned, and now there was a tension in him, a sign he was trying to regain composure, and it hurt to think that maybe he was regretting coming with me. I hesitated, giving him space to breathe, while my mind raced with worries about what had upset him so much.

Under the late evening sky, which was a deep indigo with only a few stars peeking through, my skin felt too tight.

"Okay?" I asked, which was stupid because he was obviously not okay.

"Sure," he lied, and headed toward the car, me skipping to catch up to him then falling into stride alongside him.

"Did I… was it…" Great, and there went my ability to string together sentences.

"Huh?" he asked.

"Have I upset you? Did I say or do something?" Horror struck me. "Did I choose the wrong place to take you? I should have asked you if you liked jazz, or if you wanted to go somewhere quieter." I was working myself up into a mess, and I inhaled sharply as he placed a hand on my chest.

"No, Jesus, it wasn't you."

Every line of Craig's body was rigid with strain, and it was so unlike what I'd come to learn about him—he'd relaxed with me since we were dating, loose and calm, and whatever had happened in there I wanted to go back in and fix it for him.

"My ex was in there," Craig finally said, his voice low and tight. "It didn't end well and somehow he always makes me feel..." He shrugged but I could see his expression and he was broken up about whatever had happened.

"Did he..." hurt you? hit on you? I didn't know what I was asking. He didn't know anything about my asshole ex, and I'd never asked about any of his past hookups or partners. Should we have done that by now? This was where my social skills lacked polish, but it didn't seem as if we were heading down the path of the exes discussion anyway, even though I could tell there was more to the story.

Before I could reform the question, Craig's demeanor shifted drastically from closed off to feral, and I whimpered when he pushed me against the car parked beside us and kissed me. It might have been to stop an awkward conversation, but it was a fierce, fiery kiss that spoke volumes, overflowing with all the tension and emotion he was holding back. The world narrowed down to the space where our bodies met, his tongue tangling with mine, hands gripping my jacket as if I were the only solid thing he could hold onto.

I scrambled for something to grip, laced my hands behind his head and melted into his touch. Making out in public was not something I'd done before. I'd always been reserved, cautious, calculating outcomes and potential pitfalls of discovery before I'd ever gotten to the point where people could see me. But with Craig, caution melted away under the heat of his touch. I was overwhelmed, hot as hell, and so present in the moment. Every nerve ending seemed to fire at once, every sound muffled except for the rush of my heartbeat.

As we finally broke apart, gasping for air, he seemed calmer, focused, smiling, his eyes wide, his lips damp from our kisses, and I'd forgotten there was an issue to begin with. Craig's kiss had swept away all thoughts of exes, past hurts, and bathroom confrontations. It was only him and me, here and now, the cool metal of the car contrasting with the warmth of his body.

"I've never—" I started to say, breathless, still reeling from the intensity of the moment.

Craig rested his forehead against mine, a small smile playing on his lips as he caught his breath. "Neither have I," he admitted, his eyes bright with a mix of mischief and something deeper, more honest than I'd seen in any man. I thought I'd loved Sean for his brains and his achievements, but he was nothing beside the brilliance of the man cradling me against the car.

Standing in the dimly lit street, leaning on the car with Craig's arms still around me, I felt so turned on I could have cried, and it was new, unexpected, and bloody intoxicating. Whatever fears or hesitations I had learned from exes like Sean about public displays of affection were trivial when I could be with someone like Craig. This was more than just physical attraction; it was a desperate need to be together.

"Wanna go for a drive?" he asked, then kissed me.

I hesitated, a little disappointed. Given how I was

feeling at the moment, part of me had hoped we might head back to his place or perhaps get a bit adventurous right here in the car. But the offer to drive somewhere, to extend the night in another direction, was too sweet to decline. "Sure," I replied, forcing a smile as I buckled up.

He fiddled with his playlist, setting it to a collection of soft jazz that filled the space with smooth saxophones and lazy bass lines, perfectly suiting the late-night mood, and then leaned over to kiss me.

"I wanted to take you home," he admitted.

"Okay."

He reached for my hand, and we laced our fingers, and he squeezed. "I want it to be right and I need to get my head straight."

"I understand," I said. I wished I didn't—I wished I was selfish. Post-kiss, the expectation was electric, and I wanted more.

"Thank you," he murmured, maneuvering the car onto the road. The soft jazz created a soothing backdrop, and I decided to lighten the mood with a story.

"You know, my dad used to drive me around at night to get me to sleep when I was a kid," I began, watching the city lights blur past. "He'd say it was the only way to keep me quiet for more than five minutes."

Craig chuckled, glancing my way as he drove. "Did it work?"

"Like a charm." I laughed. "But every once in a while, I'd pop my head up and ask him if we were there yet or demand another story. He'd sigh and say, 'Please, Jameson, just go to sleep.'"

Craig's laughter filled the car, a sound that made my

heart skip. "I can imagine you being that kid," he said, shaking his head.

"Hey, I was a very curious child," I defended playfully, enjoying the ease of our banter.

He hummed to the music, which was so peaceful, but then he smiled at me. "So, Jamie is short for Jameson?"

I smiled, turning to look out of the window before answering, "Yeah, Jameson Hennessy. My dad thought it clever to match the whiskey with my last name." The story always seemed to amuse people, and telling it now, in the intimacy of Craig's car, felt right—like sharing a small, personal piece of myself.

Craig chuckled. "That's cool."

He turned into a parking area underneath a sign for the Mulholland Drive lookout, and the engine's soft purr fell silent, the music stopping, and we were left with the quiet of the night.

"I love it here," he said. We stepped out, and the view was breathtaking. The city below us was a tapestry of lights and colors, vibrant even at night, alive in a way only Los Angeles can be. The lookout was peaceful, and we leaned against the car, our shoulders touching, and stared at the view. I couldn't have imagined a more perfect end to the evening, standing with Craig, high above the sprawling city, feeling like the only two people in the world.

The night air was cool, sweeping over us as we leaned against the railing, focusing on the glittering expanse of Los Angeles. Ribbons of streetlights threaded through the darkness, and the city lights blurred into one. Above, the sky was a deep velvet blue, largely obscured by the city's luminescence, yet a few stubborn stars twinkled faintly.

Craig tugged me into his side and then tucked his head into my neck. He was exactly the right height for me and perfectly fit in my arms.

Craig's voice broke through the calm, pulling me back from my reverie. "Sorry, I messed up tonight," he murmured.

"You didn't. I have a shitty ex as well, you know," I found myself saying, the cool night breeze carrying my words and regretting saying them immediately. "Shit. Sorry. Not that my shitty ex is any worse than what I assume yours was, I'm not saying that. I'm sorry."

"You love apologizing."

"It's a thing." I smirked and then shrugged.

"Tell me about your shitty ex," Craig murmured, nuzzling my throat. I could get used to having him in my arms.

"He took the credit for our shared research, and I was walking into a conference room just as the applause began, and there was Sean, soaking it all up, as if I hadn't been part of any of it. They were my theories."

"The spiral thing?"

"Yeah, and it's application. Those were my ideas, but you know what, all he has is the research, it's me who got funding, so fuck him."

"Yeah, fuck him."

"What's different between my shitty ex and your shitty ex is that I won't meet mine randomly in LA." I hesitated. "At least I hope not. He's back in New York and he'd have to be dragged to the west coast kicking and screaming." I sighed, the old frustration flaring up briefly. "I never should have stayed in New York after Oli came here but y'know, I was trying to make the boyfriend thing work. Sean was the only reason I stayed there as long as I did. And after Oli got traded here, I missed him and the girls so much and I just wanted to be with them." Craig squeezed my hand. "I want to reassure you that I will never be a shitty ex."

Craig chuckled. "You mean you don't want a full membership of the shitty exes club?"

"Nope."

"Me neither."

"Yeah, we're the good guys, right?"

"Totally." He paused. "I will tell you, if…"

If this goes any further? If he can?

I squeezed his hand. "I know."

Against the perfect backdrop of Los Angeles at night, we leaned into each other and kissed. It was deep, sweet, and hot—a kiss that felt as if it were pulling every pent-up emotion to the surface.

When we finally separated, both of us were a little breathless; Craig's eyes were bright, alive with something that looked a lot like hope. "You want to come back to my place?" he asked, with the words soft between us.

"Yes," I answered without hesitation, my voice steady despite the racing of my heart. The idea of continuing, of letting go of this connection, felt exactly right. As we headed back to his car, I couldn't help but think how perfect this night was turning out to be.

And remembering the barbecue and how hot that experience had been, I imagined the night was about to get better.

Chapter Fourteen

Craig

I HADN'T PLANNED ON THIS.

My place was a mess. Unlocking the door with Jamie at my back, I stalled after the tumblers rolled, turned, and gave him a pathetic glance.

"Okay, so, just as a warning I wasn't expecting us to be doing this tonight and I've sort of not picked up in a few days."

He took my face between his hands. "I don't care about throw pillows scattered about or the dust on the telly."

"I love you call it a telly." I loved every word he spoke.

"Whatever, Mr. Hockey. Open the door so we can get naked."

He kissed me soundly. I reached behind me, found the knob, and turned. We stumbled inside, his fingers cradling my skull, my hands coming around him to cup his ass. Mouths fused, we somehow managed to only crack our elbows on the doorframe. Hissing at the pain, we broke apart, snickering for a mere moment before falling back on each other like hungry jackals. His tongue curled around mine as I kneaded his backside through his slacks.

"Good Lord," he panted when we had to break apart so I could find the lights. "I'm this close to coming in my underwear."

I chuckled, gave his ass a good squeeze, and then took a step or two to the left to find the switch. When the room filled with light I saw his gaze flitting about as he drank in the sloppiness.

"Sorry, this is…" I hustled around my living room, picking up empty cans of soda, cheesy doodle bags, a stray sock, and a pizza box. "I have a housekeeper, really nice lady named Doris, but she's on vacation visiting her son in Killington, Vermont, where he's gotten a good job as a legal assistant. She's very proud of him." I stooped to fish some sneakers and a hockey stick out from under the sectional. "Worries he doesn't have a steady girl yet but is giving him until he's thirty-five to settle down or she's going to start looking for a nice girl for him."

"You don't have to tidy up for me, honestly. I live with two children. Chaos and things being tossed about is the norm," Jamie said as I ran about.

"I just feel funny. My mother would chew me out for bringing home a guest to a pigsty. Not that it's *that* bad, but she would think so. Mom is all about everything in its place. Oh, wait, let me move those." I dumped my armload of debris, sock, and pizza box to the floor by the kitchen and raced over to clear a space on the sofa. "You can sit here. These are just papers from the local dyslexia foundation explaining their goals and hopes for the year.

It's taking me a hot minute to get through them all. I told my sister it seems a group working for folks with learning disabilities would be less reliant on written words and use other means of communication. A short video seems like a great way to convey what they want to say, right?"

"You're completely right. Did you want to slow things down a bit?"

I gaped, papers in my hand.

Jamie continued, "It's completely fine if you've changed your mind about taking this into the bedroom."

"No! No, I haven't changed my mind at all. I just…" I let the papers flutter back to the sofa. "I really do want to take you to my bed. I was worried you'd think less of me because of the disorganization. My ex always liked to say that only the ill-educated lived in squalor."

Jamie scowled deeply. "Your ex sounds like an elitist prick."

"Yeah, he was. Still is." I sat on the couch with a huff, my shoulders sagging, the printouts crinkling under my weight. "He's a rotten person. Cruel. Seeing him tonight was a shock. I guess I shouldn't have been too surprised to run into him at a jazz club."

Jamie sat beside me after he had tossed some papers aside. He draped an arm over my shoulders, his presence calming.

"I wish you would have mentioned that. We could have met up somewhere else. I never want to put you into a situation where you might feel uncomfortable."

I gave him a wobbly smile. "That's sweet, but I can't spend my life hiding from Leon. He's a powerful lawyer in a huge law firm in LA. He's a social creature. He loves to be out and about, showing how much better he is than the commoners. Moves in big circles, represents movie stars, that kind of thing. I didn't want to make a scene. You were so excited to have me meet some of your friends. The odds that he would be there tonight were slim."

"But there he was. The bastard." He pressed a kiss to my cheek.

"Yeah, he was there, and he ruined the night. That's on me, though." I sucked in a deep breath then let it out slowly. "I shouldn't give him that kind of power. I should have marched back to the table, sat down, and kissed you passionately. I swore to myself and to my sister that I would never run from Leon again, that I would face him down, and take back the power that he stripped from me. But the first time I see him I bolt. Shit, I'm such a coward."

"You are *not* a coward. Hey, listen to me." He moved from beside me to plant his ass on the coffee table, uncaring of the fact his rump was resting on a snack-sized bag of cheese puffs. He rested his hands on my knees, his beautiful gaze grabbing mine and holding it. "You're one of the bravest men I have ever met. Only valiant souls battle through to graduate college then play in a professional sporting league." I made a face. "No, do not belittle your accomplishments, for they are mighty. You're a courageous, loving, kind man who feels deeply. Your ex is a fucking wanker. A foul, rotten maggot that feeds on those he feels are below him to boost his flaccid ego. If he ever gets into your face again, I will punch him in the nose."

That made me grin. I leaned in to press my lips to

Jamie's. "You are the sexiest thing when you've got your Brit up. Also, and this is funny in a sweet way, the fact that you the scientist who wears glasses is going to defend me, the hockey player, is making me feel all kinds of fuzzy inside."

He chortled. "Well, I might not be a pugilist, but I *will* kick the snot out of someone who hurts people I care deeply about. Granted, it might only be one cheap shot then I'll get my arse whipped…"

"They'd have to go through me to get to your arse."

"Speaking of getting to my arse…"

A jolt of desire raced through me. I pushed to stand, Jamie followed, and I offered him my hand. He slid his fingers into mine, the sizzle of his touch just as strong as it had been the first time we'd touched.

I led him to my room. The bed was a tangle of cover and sheets, and a dirty Storm hoodie hung from the closet door, but otherwise, it was tidy enough to invite a lover into. My chest was tight, my balls hot and heavy as I pulled him along to my bed. The window blinds were shut, and the small lamp on the nightstand was off until I reached out to touch the base. Then the room was filled with a soft glow. Jamie didn't look around or judge as a certain someone would have. His attention was one hundred percent on me.

"Let me undress you," I whispered and got a nod. I began with his glasses. Lifting them gently from his nose and then guiding them from his ears, I placed them on the nightstand. "You are the prettiest man I have ever met." I caressed his face, ran my fingers through his hair, and dropped small kisses on every inch of skin I exposed. His chest was pale, with only a light strip of hair leading downward. I plucked each rosy nipple, tasted, and touched the tight buds until he was short of breath. It was divine getting to know his body better. Our last time together had been so rushed—amazing for sure but rushed—so this time I wanted to spend hours learning what he liked and disliked. "Nipple play for the win?"

"God yes, huge win," he gasped.

I gave them both a flick with my thumbnails. He moaned, his hips rolling as he sought friction where there was none. Seeing how hard he was, I shifted downward, kneeling before him as I tugged the zipper on his trousers down, then eased him free of slacks, briefs, and socks. His cock rubbed over my cheek several times, leaving a wet streak of pre-cum. "If you suck me, I *will* come. I'm too close."

"Then I'll save that for later. I want you to come when I have my cock buried in your ass," I said, rising from the floor to kiss him wantonly. He clawed at my clothes, tugging madly, popping a few buttons in his haste.

When we fell into the bed nude and hard, I caged him, locked my arms, and lowered my head to claim his mouth. He was alive under me, gyrating, his prick bumping mine. My balls drew up in warning, so I slowed things down. I rolled off him, got a groan of displeasure, and then licked a wet path from his mouth to his armpit, his manly scent making it hard for me to keep things dampened.

"Lay on your belly," I urged, and he flopped over with haste. I straddled him, nestling my cock between his ass cheeks, then bent to nip and nibble his spine. His hips rolled wickedly as he ground into the bed. I rubbed his sides as I tasted him from the nape of his neck to the crack of his pert ass. "You're delicious."

"Fuck me, do it now before I lose my bloody mind," he barked as he humped the coverlet. "Do it, ravage my arse."

I would, in time, but I wanted to continue to push him closer to the edge. I wriggled down, resting my ass on his calves, and dipped my tongue into the tempting cleft between his buttocks. His pelvis jerked. He pulled at the covers until the fitted sheet popped off the corner. I licked and laved his crack, gathering spittle on my finger before pushing it between his cheeks. I found his hole. He gasped then whined. I kissed his lower back while easing the tip of my finger into his heat.

"Fuck, fuck, please… ah fucking hell that is so good!" He was so vocal. My cock throbbed with want. All I could think of was sinking into him, but I wanted him loose and ready, so I added more spit to my fingers. He lifted his stomach from the bed, offering his ass to me as if it were a platter of hors d'oeuvres. I pulled a finger out, wet it and its brother, and then pushed two digits into him, all the way in. He cried out when I found his prostate. "More, more… Craig."

There was only so much of this my aching cock could take. I eased free of his body, slapped at the nightstand like a drunken sot, and finally found the drawer. My fingers, still slick from spittle, found the lube. I glanced at my lover and groaned. His tight ass was up in the air, his face buried in my pillow, and his fingers clutching the mattress.

"You are so beautiful," I said as I coated my dick with slick.

"I'm so fucking horny," he replied, making us both laugh.

I moved behind him, took my cock in hand, and slapped his pink hole with my dick.

"Yes, that's it, sweets. Get that into me before I go mad."

"Whatever you want," I replied, then sank into him. His breathing stalled for a moment as I filled him. He inhaled sharply, the intake of air shaky as his body adjusted. Then, because he was the bossiest bottom I'd ever known, he began to roll his hips. Up onto his hands and knees, he went. I guided him back with just a few fingers on his hips. Jamie did the rest, rocking up and then back, his head hanging, his skin dewy with sweat. "You're so tight."

He murmured something I couldn't catch. I began thrusting into him, picking up the pace, pounding away madly then easing out, teasing him, leaving only the tip in. The sight of my cockhead resting in his ass pushed me over the top. I drove into him with a grunt then filled his ass. A hot wash of cum flowed out of him, down over his balls, and I felt his channel tighten, his ass milking me over and over. My cock was so sensitive I had to pull out. I eased back, just a bit, to watch my spunk drip from his nuts to the bed as his jizz mixed with mine on the rumpled sheet.

"Fuck, that is so hot," I said, my voice raspy. I ran my fingers around his rim and then down his sac, catching my spend on my index finger. As he shivered and sighed I pulled out then pushed the cum oozing out of him back inside, deep inside. Jamie cooed at the pressure then collapsed, my fingers falling free of his wet hole.

I kissed my way upward over each bump of his spine until I reached his cheek. He twisted to the side, his face ruddy and damp, and turned his head into a long, sweet, tender kiss that could have gone on forever. I know I wanted it to. I wanted forever with him. I had to believe in the goodness of Jamie's heart. So, I stepped off the proverbial ledge…

"I think I love you," I confessed with a ragged breath. Loving him was scary. The last time I'd given my heart to a man he had trampled it into the ground. I didn't think Jamie would do anything like that, he was different than Leon, I knew that. I had to learn to trust again, or I'd live a life of loneliness.

"And I love you," he whispered, rolling to his side so we could lie belly to belly in the mussed sheets to stare at each other as we made our confessions. "I will cherish you, all of you, everything about you." He pushed a few sodden strands of hair from my brow. "Will you do the same for me?"

"Always. Always. Always." I stole a kiss, then another, and then a hundred more.

Chapter Fifteen

Jamie

As I stood in the kitchen, cleaning up after a whirlwind breakfast that managed to sprawl across every conceivable surface, I stared down at the bottom of the sink, watching running water slowly swirl and spiral around the plughole. All I could think about was Craig—how being in love with him felt as if every single part of me had been changed somehow.

"Earth to Jamie, come in Jamie." Oli's voice suddenly broke through my thoughts, and I blinked, looking up to find him leaning against the kitchen counter, a bemused smile playing on his lips.

"Sorry," I chuckled, shaking my head slightly as I realized how far I had drifted. "Just thinking."

"About math?" He stared into the sink, used to me drifting away on a sea of numbers and probably wondering why the sink and the running water were my focus.

"Nope."

"About Craig?" Oli guessed, his eyebrow arching knowingly.

I nodded, feeling a warm flush spread across my cheeks. "Yeah. It's like… everything reminds me of him, even the water spiraling down the sink and the way he can do this thing with his—"

"No sex talk."

"—smile," I finished, and pressed a hand to my chest. "He smiles at me and his eyes are so… yeah… and fuck me, I'm being ridiculous."

Oli nudged my arm. "Sounds like you've got it bad. But I'm glad. He's a good guy, and you deserve someone who makes you happy."

"Thanks, Oli," I said, genuinely grateful for his support. "It feels… right, you know? Like after Sean, and the lies, it's as if everything's finally falling into place."

"Good," Oli replied, clapping me on the shoulder. "Just remember, love's supposed to lift you up, not pull you down the drain," he deadpanned.

I groaned. "That's a shit joke, mate."

"I was trying for profound," he teased and then picked up his keys. "I'm out of here."

"Say hi to Craig," I blurted and felt my skin heat. *Say hi to Craig?* What the hell was that? I could message him that. Jesus, I didn't need my best friend telling my boyfriend hi.

He nodded in all seriousness. "Do you have a note you want me to give him? Maybe with heart doodles?"

I stared at my best friend, unsure what he was asking, and then it hit me. The fucker was messing with me.

He chuckled and sidestepped the towel I flicked at him. "You're an arsehole."

He waved goodbye. "Don't forget Jackson will try to pick up the girls."

What he meant by that was I needed to be on standby in case Jackson's job got in the way. I didn't know how the three of us in the house worked, but we did. Jackson was a good guy—an annoying bastard, but a good guy. He loved Oli, and both Oli and the girls came before everything—but he didn't have control over his work life the same as Oli and I did.

"I'm around if he needs me," I said with a grin, turning off the tap and drying my hands. As I wiped down the last of the counters, I couldn't help but feel a sense of contentment with the life I was building here. Oli was looking for a new place, something to buy instead of renting, something bigger, and it didn't escape my notice that he was checking out places with more than one building on the property. He wanted me to stay, as his best friend, for the girls, and I was totally good with all of that. Happy. Add in this new thing with Craig—this love—and I was just about as happy as I'd ever been. Despite the chaos of a messy breakfast and the mundane cleaning task, my heart felt surprisingly light. Being here with my best friend, my girls, in love with Craig and thinking about him in even the smallest, most ordinary moments—it all made sense.

As if being happy was the most natural thing in the world.

With the kitchen tidied, I headed into the office. The space was half filled with boxes Oli had never unpacked, but I knew what was in them—pucks, photos, jerseys, all ready to decorate the walls of his study in his forever home. I squeezed past them and sat behind the desk, wondering if Craig had a similar collection. First goal, first hat trick, and jerseys from when he was a kid. Maybe he would have memorabilia from when he was a figure skater? I'd watched every single clip of him online, most of them shaky home videos from his parents and trainer, but it was the more recent videos that made me warm, and I pulled out a notebook, ready to take notes. I needed to do the same thing for Ian's football games and Annabelle's floor exercises, but yeah, I was obsessed with Craig.

Biased even.

Something I'd need to get a handle on. Otherwise, my data would be skewed.

But I'd do all that after I rewatched an old hockey clip on *YouTube*—highlights from a classic match where the Storm faced off against the New York Nighthawks. This particular game held a special significance for me, not just because it featured both Craig and Oli, back when Oli was still with the Nighthawks, but because this was Craig's first career hat trick, and watching him move was mesmerizing.

The game had been fierce, but Craig brought his unique flair to the game that often left traditional players like Oli grappling to keep up. His agility and finesse had been on full display that night, making him a formidable opponent even for someone as seasoned as Oli.

One moment, in particular, always stood out vividly, and it was hotter now I knew what he was like in bed. God, his confidence and competence had me so hard I could cut steel. Craig had the puck, and he was barreling toward the goal with a Nighthawk defender on his tail. Oli was in position, his stance wide, ready to intercept him. But Craig was a whirlwind on skates—his figure skating prowess shining through as he executed a perfect pirouette that bypassed Oli and left my best friend momentarily disoriented.

After spinning past Oli, Craig skated along the barrier right before the Nighthawks' bench. It was a bold, almost taunting action, his control complete as he glided effortlessly, the puck still at the tip of his stick. The crowd in the recording roared with delight, a sound that brought a smile to my face. Watching him so in control, so full of life and power on the ice, was so fucking hot.

Oli's reaction was a typical mix of frustration and reluctant respect, the latter I knew because he'd mentioned it to me once, laughing over beers about how Craig had run rings around him that night. It was funny to think of them now, teammates and friends, when they had once been adversaries on the ice.

The video was only a recording, a moment in time, yet it felt alive to me, infused with the energy and passion of the game, and that damn sexy spiral he'd used to get away from the defense.

Turning off the video, I leaned back, lost in thought about my research and what was next.

I lasted about ten minutes of academic thinking and then watched the video again.

Just once.

Well, twice, but no one was here to accuse me of shirking my responsibilities to my study.

And who the hell would comment if I happened to have it on repeat as I worked?

No one, that's who.

The first call, a harried request for help from Jackson, came in at two. He was heading into an interview room and wasn't sure when he'd be out. I set an alarm to pick up the girls and was nearly done with figuring out why my phone wasn't using a twenty-four-hour clock, when the damn thing rung again. Jackson again, telling me he was going to be half an hour later than the first time he gave me and not to forget.

"I won't forget!" I muttered. I'd never shirked my responsibility to the girls, and I'd been doing it way longer than him.

When the phone rang a third time I flicked the call up and put it on loudspeaker.

"I said I'm on it, arsehole. Stop checking up on me."

Silence, then the sound of someone who was decidedly not Jackson, clearing their throat. I glanced at the screen and my heart fell. Barbara Millstone from the University Grants Commission, and I'd just called her, or Jackson anyway, an arsehole.

"Umm, Dr. Hennessy?" she said with caution.

Shit. Shit. Shit.

"Sorry, I thought you were someone else. Sorry." I apologized twice—I mean, a man can never apologize enough, right?

"Okay," she said, but she didn't sound warm, and my chest got all squirrelly then tight. "I've had some feedback on the initial reports you submitted, and a couple of the board have some concerns."

Concerns? Already? All they'd had so far was my initial groundwork, hypothesis, and background. I'd covered every base, analyzed the potential income that could be generated by my study should they choose to sell it on to teams. Only last season, a football team in Montana had paid out seventeen million to a company for how they could optimize grass for god's sake. My research was bigger than that.

More than that.

"Okay…" I prompted.

"A letter was received from a company out of New York, umm… OberonTech… who suggested your study is based on existing research, and I want your side of this, so I know what to say to them."

OberonTech.

OberonTech, who'd paid Sean a metric ton of money for what was my research.

I could hardly believe what I was hearing; the audacity was staggering. I was embarrassed, furious, and, above all, determined to set the record straight.

Keep calm.

"This is nonsense," I began.

"Still, I need to take this seriously, Dr. Hennessy."

"As do I," I said. "I will get you a letter of retraction immediately, Barbara," I promised, my voice steady despite the turmoil swirling inside me. I knew what I had to do next—I had to confront Sean face-to-face, even if only through a digital screen.

Setting up the call, I tried to steel myself against the emotions churning through me. When his face appeared on my screen, smug and irritatingly calm, a part of me wanted to reach through the monitor and shake the truth out of him.

"Well hello there, sweetness," he said, all smiles as if this were a social call.

"Don't call me that."

He pouted. Fake-pouted. How did I ever find this man attractive? Now I had Craig in my life and my heart, it highlighted how unattractive Sean was. Not just how he faked his way through life, but in the darkness of his dead heart. What kind of mathematician fudges results, tells lies, and steals research?

A Moriarty level of an evil fucking arsehole, that's who.

"What did you do?" I asked, and he knew exactly what I meant.

"Just set the record straight," he said, all oily and pouty.

I wanted to reach through the screen and punch his oily, pouty face.

"How about you come back to New York, Jamie? We can work this out together," Sean offered smoothly, as if it were the most reasonable suggestion in the world. "I'll even put your name back on your... on the research."

"No, Sean," I replied, my voice cold and hard. "I'm not returning to New York, and I'm certainly not working with you. Not now, not *ever*." The finality of my words seemed to take him by surprise, his smug expression faltering just a bit.

"There's no need for rudeness, sweetheart."

"I am not your sweetheart."

"You know I wouldn't intentionally hurt you with this, but—"

"Fuck. You," I snapped and promptly snorted a laugh when he clutched some imaginary pearls. I don't think I'd ever pulled out that curse with him—maybe I should have done so way before this.

His indignation turned sly. "You just have to come back…"

"Not happening."

He shrugged then as if he wasn't messing with my life. "That's your choice."

I glanced away from him and found the file I'd kept safe. I dragged it into the chat window and heard the noise of it arriving at his end.

"What's this?" he asked, still smiling, until he read the file I'd cleverly named *SeanIsAWanker.docx*. "What the hell—"

"Open it."

He muttered something, and I saw his gaze slip to wherever the file had opened on the screen. I gave him five.

Four.

Three.

Two.

One.

"What the fuck did you do, Jamie?" he yelled.

"I think the data is clear."

"Jamie—"

"Behold the vast amount of fuckery you enacted on the data to mold it to suit the results you wanted."

He stared right at me, and horror turned to smugness.

"You release this, then it's your name against what we did."

"*We* didn't do anything," I replied, dragging another file into the chat called *JamieIsNotAWanker.docx*. I'd never seen Sean move so fast as he opened it. "See, that is the original data that we were submitting before you changed it. Now, my name is no longer on this study, and we both know what you did exposed flaws, and it has to be started all over again."

"You arsehole—"

"Nope, that would be you," I muttered. Then I leaned closer to the camera, my resolve hardening. "And unless you retract your accusations, I won't just allow this to fade in the background while you start again; I will expose the manipulation of data you conducted during this project. I might have taken the hit with my research because you removed me from the project, but you have shown me the kind of man you were, and I'm relieved you fucked me over."

He was stuck somewhere between arrogant and horrified. "You won't reveal shit," he snarled. "You're way too polite to embarrass yourself by admitting you knew what I'd done."

There it was, that smug shit again. "I'm way past being embarrassed, and I've sent out enough emails to ensure what you have means nothing. With great regret, I've hinted in every message that I feel the data collection was flawed."

"You fuck—"

"—And I will release the raw data that shows it was all

you." I leaned to one side, tapping at my keyboard. He didn't have to know I was faking typing an email.

Sean's face went pale, the smugness evaporating. "You wouldn't dare," he snarled, his veneer of control slipping.

"I would, and you know I will. If you take away the work I'm doing here, if you undermine me in any way, then I have nothing to lose anymore, Sean," I said firmly. The threat hung between us, heavy and dangerous.

After a moment of tense silence, he nodded slowly, beaten. "Fine."

"Send a retraction to the commission. Do it now. I'll wait."

"Now, be reasonable. I'll send it as soon as this call is ended."

"Copy me in. You have ten minutes, or I send this evidence email to OberonTech, NYU, and the University Grants Commission." I ended the call abruptly, feeling neither triumph nor relief, only a weary resignation. The victory, if it could be called that, was hollow, tainted by the fact I'd had to pull out the big guns.

The email from him, copying me in, arrived within five minutes, full of excuses and accusations of misunderstandings, and I forwarded it on to Barbara.

I sat back in my chair, startled when my alarm sounded. The girls.

I was at the school within twenty minutes, not entirely recalling the journey. The burn of righteous indignation was strong in my chest, and I had to watch the Craig video three times before I calmed down.

Scarlett and Daisy were a breath of fresh air, talking, demanding, laughing, and taking my mind off everything.

Barbara's email arrived a short time after we got home, acknowledging that the situation was resolved.

Damn right it was resolved.

Then Jackson was there, armed with a supply of Cadbury chocolate—his usual apology for me having to step in. I didn't have the heart to tell him it wasn't the same as the chocolate back home, because I wasn't mean like that.

Then Oli arrived, Craig trailing after him. I snagged Craig as soon as I was able, tugging him into the study and shutting the door.

Our reunion was all kisses and sighs, and him telling me he loved me, and me saying it back. Between breaths, I announced my small victory, "I won my battle of the exes today," letting the relief and triumph spill over into our kissing.

Someone knocked loudly on the door. "Break it up guys! Pizza is here!"

We broke it up, but not before several more kisses, and by the time we made it to the kitchen, nearly all the best slices were gone. I didn't care because I had Craig, kisses, and love.

However, the peace was short-lived. Midway through a joke Jackson was cracking about his work partner, Craig's phone vibrated harshly against the kitchen countertop. He excused himself with a tight smile and stepped into the yard to take the call. I tried to focus on the joke, but part of me was tuned to the muffled cadence of Craig's voice drifting through the slightly open door, the tone tight and worried.

Craig's expression was stiff, his face drawn, the earlier

ease gone, replaced by a tension in him that knotted his shoulders. I caught the weight of Oli's stare, and we exchanged shrugs before I excused myself, following Craig outside.

"Craig?" I kept my voice low, but it was laced with concern, as I reached out to touch his arm. He turned to me, his expression taut, a forced smile not quite reaching his eyes. "What's wrong?"

"It's nothing I can't handle," he finally said, though his voice betrayed the strain of whatever news the call had brought. I knew better than to push. I really did, but I loved him, and I didn't want to see him so sad.

"A problem shared…" I prompted and took his hands in mine. "Is it the team?" My heart sank. "Are you being traded?" What if he was traded somewhere miles from here, away from Oli and the girls? What would I choose? Where would I go?

Why was I being asked to decide this when being in love with Craig was so new?

"No, it's not the team."

"Then what?"

He closed his eyes and rested his forehead on mine. "I have no idea where to start."

Chapter Sixteen

Craig

IF I COULD BE HONEST WITH ANYONE, IT WAS WITH JAMIE.

Still, even knowing that, it took me several minutes to force the secrets that I'd kept bottled up inside me to spill. They leaked out in a small dribble at first, both of us seated on the swings of the redwood play fort in the backyard.

"I'm sorry," I said for the twelfth time in forty seconds. My thoughts were a jumbled word gumbo, and I felt like a toddler trying to pick out the letters to spell garbage from his bowl of alphabet soup. Because if any descriptor of things right now in my life fit it was garbage. Maybe terror. "I just…" I blew out a breath, rubbed my face with my palms, and then locked my legs to stop the swing from moving. "My sister had a phone call from my ex."

I peeked to the side to see Jamie trying to connect the dots and failing. "Why would he call your sister?"

And here it was. The place where all the refuse

tumbled out onto the street for the world to step over, or kick into the sea.

"She has Bruno."

Jamie also stopped swinging. "Is Bruno your son?" His voice was shaky now.

"No, no, Bruno is my dog."

His exhalation was legendary. "Okay, well, that's a completely different scenario. I didn't know you owned a dog. So, tell me about Bruno and why Leon the Horror is calling *your* sister about *your* dog."

I swallowed down the worry. "Leon gave me Bruno as a gift for our first anniversary. He was the cutest little puppy. He has to wear little sweaters because he's a Chinese Crested. He's the hairless variety and gets cold easily. He's a smart dog but excitable and gets anxious when he senses upset in his people. Leon said he was a sound investment and would give me something to talk about when we were among his colleagues. Guess I was too stupid to talk about anything other than a dog."

"I loathe your ex increasingly with every passing hour," Jamie mumbled while maneuvering to the right to rub my bowed back. "It sounds like you love Bruno a lot."

"I do, and he got me through some really terrible times. When I left I took Bruno with me. He was mine, and I honestly didn't trust Leon alone with the dog. I was scared he would take out his anger on him. One kick would probably kill him, he's just a little dog." A shudder ran through me just thinking of it. "When I left, I went home to Michigan and stayed with Claudia in her small apartment. Bruno was a wreck, nerved up, scared of this new house and this woman he barely knew. Leon found us right off, began calling all the time, both Claudia and me, begging at first, imploring me to come home to him. We'd work things out, he said. When I said no he started texting me instead of calling. I changed my number several times. Claudia moved to a new house with a yard that I helped her finance. Leon never stopped texting me, somehow he always found my number and where I lived no matter how often I moved."

Jamie pulled me into his side, the chains on the swings creaking under our weight. "God what a controlling bastard he is. We both really did shit the bed on our previous choices, didn't we?"

"Yeah, you could say that. Every month, at least twice, he texts me asking me to reconsider. Telling me that if I'd only stop being so hysterical, I'd see we were destined to be together. I used to reply to the texts, but that only brought more lies, so I just ignore them now. I keep them on my phone, though. Is that weird?"

"No—"

"I'm scared, and that's stupid, right?"

Someone cleared their throat, and we both whirled to find Jackson at the back door. "Sorry, I wasn't listening in, but uhm... I'm tuned into these conversations, and I was in the kitchen, and I could hear you and, jeez..." He dipped his head in embarrassment. "Why are you scared of your ex?"

I lifted my chin. He wouldn't be the first person who said I was a grown man and shouldn't fear Leon. Hell, I thought the same thing myself.

"He has every right to be scared," Jamie defended me.

Jackson raised his hands in defense. "Of course he

does. Look, I'm sorry for overhearing your conversation but, do you want me to sit in on this talk? If you don't want me here that's fine, Craig, but from a cop's perspective what I heard made me nervous."

I glanced at Jamie. He knew Jackson much better than I did. Jamie nodded softly. "He's an annoying asshole but a good cop." He sounded begrudging, but I could see they were friends, and he was probably teasing.

Jackson fake-swooned. "Jamie just called me a good cop."

It lightened the mood a little, and yeah, there was something in Jackson I thought I could trust. I didn't want to involve the cops, but he was the friend of a friend, and maybe he could give me kind of legal advice.

"Sure, you can sit in, I guess." I sighed. "But Leon hasn't done anything illegal."

"I'm not sure that's true," Jackson said, sitting on the end of the slide, shoulders slouched, elbows on knees, and giving me a kind smile. "Can you start at the beginning again?"

This talk suddenly felt very different. Did I want to discuss this with a cop? Leon had never threatened me with physical harm. Never hit me. What did Jackson think he could add to this nightmare? Jamie hugged me a little tighter. The tale of Craig and Leon began again. From our meeting at a legal fund benefit for the homeless of LA to our whirlwind romance to my moving in with him a mere three months after we'd met. Leon was charming, rich, so damn smart, stylish. Everything I felt I wasn't. I wanted to absorb his confidence by osmosis or something, I guess. To this day I can't put my finger on why I'd allowed myself to be so easily manipulated.

I touched on how things at home, once he had me in his space, began to shift from Leon being the kind man to being the critical lover over the course of several months. It had been a slow progression. I'd barely noticed it, but the longer I was with him, the lower my self-confidence sank. Claudia saw it, though, and she made it known that she didn't like Leon or his treatment of her brother to anyone who would listen. And several dozen who didn't want to listen but had been forced to.

"And maybe that is on me? Maybe because I think of myself as less, I allowed him to make me feel that way."

"No!" Jamie defended, "That's bullshit."

Jackson said little as the flow of memories increased from a trickling stream to a torrential dousing that could sweep a small town off the side of a mountain. All the nitpicking, the slights, the public humiliations all gushed out of me. Two years of being belittled had finally worn me down.

"Then one night, it all came to a head. He was late for dinner with one of his clients. I had a hockey game. He came unglued, called me a moron for putting a stupid game before his needs, and stormed out after taking a swing at Bruno napping on our bed."

"He hit your dog?"

"He missed, but that one backhanded attempt was it for me, because if he could pick on something as helpless as a tiny dog…"

I leaned into Jamie, who tightened his hold as he muttered several choice curses.

I continued, "I'd been called a moron or retarded or a dimwit my whole life but that night... I don't know. He'd called me far worse over our time together, but him lifting a hand to a tiny dog who loved us both unconditionally... that I wasn't going to stand for. I packed up Bruno and my clothes, and I left Leon. My coach at the time was unhappy with me calling up and saying I had a family crisis, but he gave me a few days off to get things organized. When I got back to Michigan, my folks were surprised to see me, I'd never told them about the shit with Leon or what he'd done to Bruno. I was too ashamed. I bunked with my sister, who knew the reality of things, and when I returned to New York, I left Bruno with Claudia. I assumed after she moved, Leon had lost track of her. I prayed he had, but he's obviously found her."

Jackson sighed hard, muttering something about the internet. "It's not hard to track someone down if you're diligent. He's a lawyer, right?"

"Yeah."

"Then his firm probably has a private investigator on staff. Easy enough to follow you when you went home for the summer. He might have had that info months ago and sat on it until he needed it," Jackson said, his brow furrowed as he spoke. "You said you kept all the texts he's sent you?"

"Yeah, I have them in a folder. It's stupid..."

"No, not at all. They're evidence."

"Look, I know I don't have all the facts here, but to me, this sounds like a case of cyberstalking."

"But he's not following me around or anything," I argued.

"He doesn't have to. Cyberstalking is a pattern of behavior unwanted by the victim, that leaves the person being stalked feeling afraid or in danger. The messages and the texts don't have to be direct threats to you or your loved ones, or your dog, but if any of it makes you feel scared in any manner, then it's a case of cyberstalking. For a man who seems to think he's so damn smart, it seems he should know better. Sometimes, the smartest folks are the dumbest when it comes to common sense. No slight intended, Jamie."

"None taken," Jamie said. "I wholly agree. Some of the most intelligent people I know are thick as shit when it comes to common sense."

I sat there dumbfounded.

"Thing is… he is clever, and a lawyer, and he's said that he would take me to court for Bruno. That he has the ownership papers and that no judge would rule in my favor. I can't let him have Bruno. He's not a dog person. Hell, he's not a people person! He only wants the dog as a bargaining chip and to drive a stake into my heart, as if all the slights and name-callings over our relationship hadn't hurt me bad enough."

"We will *not* let him get his hands on Bruno. Surely there must be some legal recourse," Jamie stated, his arms tight around me.

"Are the papers really in his name?" Jackson asked.

I nodded.

His frown didn't lift my spirits.

"Okay, well, that's something to battle out with lawyers, sadly, but if we can gather enough evidence of cyberstalking, we could possibly hold that over his head if he does want to take things that far. I have some buddies in the cybercrimes department. If you want to talk with them to see if the texts can be used to possibly build a case against Leon then I'd be happy to sit in with you on your meeting. Also, if you can list the gifts with approximate dates and what they meant to you, that would help."

"Okay." I sounded so unsure.

"It's totally up to you. Your call. I'm not going to push you to do anything. But remember that most stalkers don't relent until law enforcement is involved. And even then, many are so obsessed they still can't stop. This man seems to be quite smart. Perhaps a long talk with the cops or the Feds, who take any cybercrime quite seriously, will get him to back off. Whatever you decide, you can come to me anytime to discuss this situation. I'm always happy to pay a visit to a bully. People respond well to my little chats with them. It's my stunning personality."

Jamie snorted.

I had to smile.

"Thanks, I... I don't know what to do. Claudia recorded Leon's threat. Maybe I should call Leon and tell him not to speak to my sister ever again?" Jamie threaded his fingers into my hair, a soft touch that worked wonders. "Would that help?"

Jackson shook his head. "I'd advise not to reply to him in any form." He pushed up from the slide onto his bare feet. "If he knows that he's rattled you, then he'll just do it again. Did your sister tell him never to contact her again?"

"She said she told him to take a long walk off a very short fucking pier," I replied. Both men chuckled. A smile pulled at the corner of my mouth. "Claudia is tiny but mighty. Kind of like Bruno. Do you think he can take my dog back?" Neither of them said anything, meaning they secretly felt I didn't have a leg to stand on. "Shit, shit, shit."

"Let's not panic," Jamie said, and Jackson gave me a meager smile before heading back inside. The screen door closed softly, and a moth battered itself against the muted yellow light on the back porch.

"I'm trying not to."

"I'm sure this will all be sorted one step at a time. I think you need to decide if you're willing to take this to the police or not."

"If I don't do something, it's just going to keep happening, or he will move on his threat to take me to court over Bruno, which will also bring our personal lives into the public light. What if all of this is public and it hits social media and my career... what if..."

"Don't dwell on the what-ifs."

"Ugh, I wish he would just leave me the hell alone!"

"He will. We'll end this one way or another. Just know that if you do have to go public, I will be right at your side. Fuck Leon and his manipulations. What a massive wanker. What kind of bellend threatens to take a dog away from its happy home?"

"I love it when you get all riled up and your Brit flows free."

"*Rule Britannia, Britannia rules the waves,*" Jamie sang with a mock flag wave. I snuggled into his side, my swing seat digging painfully into my hockey player's ass. Even with my ass being pinched by hard wood, there was nowhere else I would rather be than in this backyard with the warm California winds moving over us, my head on my lover's shoulder.

Seemed I had some major decisions to make before the morning light hit the Pacific Ocean.

I SPENT THAT NIGHT WITH JAMIE IN HIS BED, WRAPPED around him, wide awake as he slept. The house was quiet, the Santa Ana winds blowing the sheers on the open window. The sound of the man I loved sleeping soundly helped me focus. Hours passed, me in the dark, Jamie out like a light, as I went over every small detail of my relationship with Leon Schmied. I watched the sunrise on Jamie's bare back, the pinks of another glorious day in paradise tinting his ivory skin the color of a peony. Pressing a kiss to his shoulder, I eased out of bed, pulled on the same clothes I'd worn last night, and made my way into the kitchen.

Jackson was sitting at the counter, hair mussed, dressed in a wrinkled blue shirt, dark blue slacks, and a tie with tiny pink dots on it. He cradled a cup of coffee as the pot dripped steadily into a Minnie Mouse thermos.

"You look like shit," he said casually, between slurps of dark roast.

"Right back at you," I tossed out, then leaned against the fridge. "Would you be free today to talk to your friends in the cybercrimes department?"

He stared at me for a long minute over his cup of coffee. "I have court this morning, but maybe after lunch?" I nodded. "I'll give Joanne and Mike a call. They're good people. Joanne is a wild child, you'll like her. She has little dogs, too. Carries them to parties in a purse. I asked her once if she was substituting dogs for dicks. She laughed so hard she peed herself but did, in fact, substantiate that she would much rather spend time with a poodle than ninety percent of the men she'd ever met."

"Guess we're the lucky ones. We've found some great guys."

"Yeah, we did, but we had to kiss a shit ton of frogs first, eh?"

Boy, that was the most truthful statement I had ever heard. I still had warts on my soul from kissing Leon…

Chapter Seventeen

Jamie

I COULDN'T BELIEVE IT HAD BEEN FIFTY-THREE DAYS SINCE Craig and I had had our first date.

Not that I was counting, but my maths brain never stopped, and I could count all the ways we made each other happy.

We'd moved from one high to another, the most recent being shower sex, which I never thought possible from a mechanical point of view, but I was very happy to be proven wrong. I was still on a high from what Craig had managed to achieve. I stood at the front of the small conference room, laser pointer in hand, ready to present the summary of my findings to a group that had expanded well beyond my original circle of three subjects—Craig, Annabelle, and Ian. Now the group included independent and voluntary coaches from various disciplines, not just hockey, football, and gymnastics, but also soccer and baseball. The expansion reflected the growing interest and potential application of my research.

Or at least that was why they were here, but I'd

summarized my hypothesis as "making things better with data" to attract their attendance. Craig had been up with me last night, running me through my presentation, asking me why on so many occasions—why does that have to be a slide? Why is that so hard for you to explain? Why don't we kiss some more?

He'd made me rethink this presentation in so many ways—and even though he joked about dumbing it down, which earned him a thorough kissing, what he meant was that if people didn't understand what I was doing, then what was the point of doing it?

"Explain it like real life," he said.

And then in bed.

And in the shower this morning.

And just before this presentation started.

As I clicked through the slides, outlining the data and our methodological approaches, my voice steady and confident, I couldn't help but let my gaze drift to the back of the room. There, in a shadowed corner, sat Craig. His presence was like a magnetic pull, drawing my attention despite the moment's importance.

He was leaning back in his chair, arms crossed, a slight smile playing on his lips as he followed the presentation. Every so often, he would nod slightly, his eyes reflecting pride and perhaps a hint of amusement at my barely concealed nervousness. Seeing him so relaxed and supportive filled me with a warmth that offset the cool, professional air.

It made me feel as if I could yank all this data from its theory stage and actually make something real from it.

Despite my best efforts to focus on the audience as a

whole—most of whom were attentive—my gaze invariably wandered back to Craig. His confidence, and the subtle encouragement in his beautiful smile, grounded me. Somehow he reassured me that the path I was on was the right one, and hell, each glance at him smoothed any tremor in my voice and kept me from spiraling into stats and theorems.

I touched on the theoretical aspects and glanced at the data trends on the large screen, but all the while, my heart was anchored at the back of the room where Craig sat. The discussion shifted from statistical analysis to potential real-world applications, and I fielded questions from a football coach curious about injury prediction and a gymnastics instructor interested in motion efficiency.

As the session drew to a close, I summarized our next steps and expressed gratitude for their contributions and feedback. Polite applause filled the room, and conversations began to buzz as small groups formed to discuss the implications further.

I made my way to the back of the room, my professional mask giving way to a more genuine smile as I approached Craig. His approval meant more to me than any accolade the academic or sports community could offer. The connection we shared, filled with love and respect for each other's passions, was the cornerstone of my current happiness and future ambitions.

"Great job, Doc," Craig whispered as I reached him, his hand finding mine, giving it a reassuring squeeze. His simple praise, delivered with a warm smile, was everything.

"Let's hope the funding is approved for the next stage," I murmured.

"It will be."

"Dr. Hennessy?" A young woman with a high ponytail rested her hand on Craig's arm and leaned past him to see me. I smiled at her, adopting the polite and encouraging demeanor Craig jokingly insisted was essential. A former Olympic gymnast, Emmy-Lou Fontaine was now a coach here at the college, responsible for Annabelle's training. She was known for her enthusiasm and her keen interest in applying theoretical data to practical coaching.

"Hello," I said after a pause.

"Can I steal you for a moment? I have several questions…" I noticed her pale pink polished nails against the fabric of Craig's Storm jacket—an innocent touch, yet a spike of unexpected jealousy jabbed at me. Without overthinking, I leaned in and kissed Craig square on the lips, marking a moment of impulsiveness that was rare for me. Only then did I allow myself to be dragged away.

He grinned at me for my stupidly possessive move.

I loved that smile.

"How can I help you?" I asked when I'd been dragged a sufficient distance away from Craig that I started to want to go straight back. Emmy-Lou launched into her questions, detailing her thoughts on how my research could be integrated into her gymnastics training regimen. As we talked—and after I chilled a lot more—I found my focus drifting back to Craig, seeing him laugh in the crowd and his ease among people. It was one of the many reasons I found myself so drawn to him, and as I engaged in a technical discussion with Emmy-Lou, part of me was always tethered back to him, to us.

He was not like anyone I'd been with before.

He was mine.

I was his.

"… so that was my intention. What do you think?"

I blinked at Emmy-Lou. "Sorry, I was distracted, can you summarize that last part?"

She was so patient, repeated it all, and I really focused. Mostly.

By the time the presentation ended, and everyone had left, bar Craig who was kicked back in a seat by the door, I was on a high. The commission couldn't accuse me of not delivering, and I had a solid basis for what could be years of research into practical applications of my theories and could earn good money.

I might be able to afford a house of my own.

Or not.

I loved living with Oli and the girls, and Jackson had never implied he didn't want me there, but still… somewhere for me and Craig? Somewhere with a place where Claudia could live with us, and Bruno, of course. Next door to Oli. That seemed reasonable.

Right?

A FEW DAYS LATER, JACKSON FOUND ME IN THE GARDEN, where I was deep in conversation with Scarlett and Daisy about the merits of pink dresses as Scarlett made me try on lip glosses and Daisy attempted to keep my hair back with a flowery headband. I grinned up at the man, but he didn't seem as if he'd come out to tease me over the hair or the makeup, instead, he had a face like thunder. Fuck. What was wrong?

"Jamie, can I have a moment?" he asked, glancing at the girls before focusing his intense gaze back on me.

"Sure, what's up?" I replied, keeping my tone even, standing from my crouch. Even though I stayed calm, thinking about the girls, they reacted to Jackson's aura and paused their excited chatter. "It's okay, girls, go inside, I bet I'm just in trouble for messing with J's breakfast this morning."

"Wait!" Jackson said, with fake horror, playing to the girls. "What did he do to my breakfast?"

I leaned into Scarlett and Daisy. "I put sugar in his coffee!"

They snickered, and we all smiled, but Jackson's and my smile dropped after they'd dashed inside.

"What's wrong?" I demanded. "Is Oli okay—"

"It's Craig," Jackson began, his voice low, and my chest tightened. "He received a *gift*, and my colleagues out of cybercrimes got the call from him and said he's spooked. They gave me a courtesy call, and I'm heading out there, but maybe Craig might need a friend right now."

"Of course, I'll go," I said without hesitation, the concern for Craig overpowering. I thought that shit had stopped, but maybe it hadn't? Had Craig decided not to tell me if he was getting gifts? I quickly scrubbed my face, and followed Jackson to his car, catching sight of the headband and taking it off. "Is he okay?"

"I don't know—she didn't say much."

"But he's not hurt." I had all these scenarios where that ex-arsehole had sent him anthrax in the post, or poison, or... fuck knows.

"No medics were called out," was all he said, and that meant nothing. Craig was just like Oli, a stubborn ass over any kind of injury.

The drive to Craig's place was tense, filled with an uneasy silence that I didn't want to break with too many questions when Jackson's focus remained on the road, his jaw set in a firm line. I spent the ride trying to prepare myself for whatever situation awaited us, but as we approached Craig's residence, a modest three-bedroom house tucked neatly behind a high wall with a security gate, my anxiety heightened. The presence of a black and white cop car parked outside his front door did nothing to ease my nerves. A woman stood to the left of the entrance, her body language tense as she spoke to a young guy who was gesticulating wildly.

"I just delivered it! I just delivered it! I don't know!" the young man was defending, agitated but not angry.

"Who's the woman?" I asked quietly as we neared the front door, noting how her demeanor was relaxed as she spoke, calming the man down.

"That's Detective Joanne Russo. Cybercrimes. She's been handling the situation with the messages to Craig with her partner," Jackson whispered, scanning the area for any sign of threat. The detective gave Jackson a nod, and then indicated we should go into the house.

When we walked into Craig's living room, the scene was grimly surreal. On the coffee table, a cake shaped unmistakably like Craig's dog, Bruno, complete with a tiny, frosted jumper, lay in two pieces. What looked like jam or red icing was smeared grotesquely in and around the split, a macabre sight that made my stomach churn.

I focused on finding Craig and ensuring he was okay. Leaving the police with the cake, I had to look through several rooms but finally found him in the kitchen, with his back to me, staring out of the window.

"Craig!"

He spun to face me. "Jamie? What are you doing here?"

"Jackson said you needed me, I'm here."

Craig shrugged and didn't reach for me, as if he was holding himself back, and I held out a hand—it was up to him if he came to me, I wouldn't push my fear onto him.

"He's insane," Craig snapped, and then something changed, and he grabbed my hand and buried his face in my neck. "Fucking insane."

"Your sister?"

"Okay, she's okay."

"And Bruno?"

"He's okay too," he assured me, then gestured toward the living room where the cake sat, a tech now hovering over it, taking photos. "But this... this gift was sick. Cybercrimes are dealing with it."

I held him in a tight embrace and felt him stiffen before he relaxed slightly against me. "I won't let this get to me," he murmured, his voice muffled against my shoulder. "I have a game tonight. You're still coming, right?"

The concern in his question tugged at me. "Of course, I'm coming. But should you be playing?" I asked, pulling back just enough to look him in the eye, searching for any sign that he might be pushing himself too hard. But there was my hockey guy, my nothing-stops-me-playing guy. The man I loved.

Craig's jaw set, determination blazing in his eyes as he met my gaze squarely. "Damn right I will," he affirmed, the fierceness in his tone leaving no room for argument.

I nodded, understanding. "Then I'll be there, cheering the loudest," I promised, squeezing his hands.

The cake and its box were removed, the cop car left, and Detective Russo reassured us they would leave no stone unturned in finding out who was doing this. She didn't mention Leon's name, but we all knew. Only Jackson remained, leaning against the inside of the front door as if stopping anyone from getting in.

I smiled at him.

He nodded at me, then added a tender look.

Jackson was taking this personally, and that was what Craig needed.

CRAIG HAD FOREGONE HIS USUAL AFTERNOON PREPARATION for tonight's game, which he told me mostly included carbing up and then sleeping for an hour. Instead, we cuddled in his bed, and when he had to go to the arena, we split, and I called a cab to go home.

Not before the sweetest goodbye kiss, though.

As I walked hand in hand with Scarlett and Daisy, both girls decked out in their adorable LA Storm outfits, ready for the seven o'clock game against Montreal, I couldn't help the rush of anticipation of seeing Craig play in the flesh. The girls were bubbling with excitement, chattering about the players they were going to see and the game. Their enthusiasm was infectious, reminding me of the first time I'd done this back in New York. But now, everything felt different.

New York had been mixed with too many memories of Oli losing Melissa, a time clouded by grief and adjustment. Not to mention me putting everything into trying to make things work with Sean and then losing access to all my data.

LA represented a fresh start, one that none of us had seen coming but all desperately needed. Here, not only had Oli found a new sense of home with the LA Storm and met his man, but I'd also fallen for Craig, and my love for him was something so damn pure and uplifting; it felt as though every day with him brought a new reason to smile.

Oli still hadn't asked Jackson to marry him, and I was sure he was waiting for the perfect moment. The two of them, plus the girls, of course, had plans to go to Disneyland for two whole days for Scarlett's upcoming eighth birthday, and I couldn't help but speculate about a possible proposal. Maybe Oli would pop the question on Dumbo the Flying Elephant, or perhaps under the twinkling lights of It's a Small World—both places seemed fitting for such a magical moment when you had two children with you who were going to be part of the entire proposal.

Whatever Oli's plans were, it meant that I was all Craig's for the next two nights. With no games or traveling to get in the way, I was heading to Craig's place right after the game tonight, and then it was only the two of us for a whole two nights and one entire day. No babysitting, no working—just us.

We'd planned hot tub time, sex time, cuddling time, but maybe none of that would happen now.

I'd be happy with just the cuddling.

I simply wanted to be with him.

Chapter Eighteen

Craig

BUBBLES, BUBBLES EVERYWHERE.

Jamie and I were chin-deep in the hot tub sipping some clementine-flavored sparkling water with the stars twinkling above us. This soak under the waning moon was just what we needed. Two days alone with no hockey—thank you NHL schedulers—no kids, no housemates, and most of all no texts from Leon. He'd been incredibly quiet since the cake incident. Probably plotting his legal strategy to battle my claims in court. His position in his law firm had been terminated within days of a visit from the police to *"discuss"* this situation with him in his office situated oh so politely on Wilshire Boulevard in a modern glass building. I could only assume the news had traveled like a flu bug through the forty-plus attorneys in that building.

"You're a few thousand miles away," Jamie commented, bringing me back from my ex and his wrangling to avoid being labeled a stalker.

"Sorry." I smiled over at him, a soft wind blowing over my damp cheeks to tickle the wet hair on the nape of my neck. "I was thinking about Leon."

"What's he done now? Has he changed his mind about representing himself in court?"

"No, oh God no. He's far too narcissistic to think anyone but him could provide him with proper representation in court." Jamie rolled his eyes to the slip of a moon. "I know his ego knows no bounds. More power to him. I think we have him pretty well dead to rights on the stalking charge. The texts will prove that, as well as the cake, even if he is claiming that the cake was a gift to me to celebrate our beloved Bruno's third birthday."

"Yeah, no judge in the world is going to believe there was no malicious intent."

"You know he's the smartest man in the universe. Surely the judge will buy into his claim that he knew I adored red velvet cake and that was why the inside of the cake was scarlet. And how could it possibly be his fault that the bakery delivery fumbled the cake, breaking it in half, and smearing frosting about. Surely no one can fault him for poor service from the bakery."

Jamie frowned. "He might be able to get that one past a judge. Is red velvet your favorite?" I nodded. "Damn. Was the cake ordered to be in two chunks?"

"The baker claims it was one solid cake when it left his shop, picked up by someone he doesn't remember."

"Well, that sucks." He shifted a little closer, being sure to keep his glass of clementine fizz above the bubbling water.

"It does. And the driver who delivered the cake has mysteriously disappeared after talking to the cops. Just quit after that first day. All his info on his application was false so we have one flimsy description from the bakery owner that we handed over to the cops and a PI to hopefully track him down. It's just so mentally exhausting."

"Why would someone hire someone without checking his background and such?"

"The guy was strapped, and he was supposedly a friend of a friend, so he took the chance. The friend of a friend was also BS, but the delivery man knew enough about the baker to know some of his friends. It's all really creepy, which fits Leon well."

I was so grateful to have a restraining order in place now. I should have done it long ago, but I kept hoping Leon would move on with his life and leave me to do the same.

"Honestly, is there no depths of evil conduct that arsehole won't sink to?"

I refused to dwell on the whole who-owned-Bruno aspect of this mess. Yes, his name was on the registration papers. But the cake incident and my testimony about him trying to hit the dog was, I prayed, going to be enough to bring him down in court. If they granted ownership to Claudia that would be fine with me. Sure, I'd love to have my dog back, but he was happy with my sister. If Leon was granted custody of Bruno I might do something rash, and it would be *me* facing charges. If only he would relent about taking Bruno. I would have settled out of court—

hell, all I wanted was for him to leave me the fuck alone, screw any monetary damages that might come to me—but oh no, he had to *"expunge the heinous slights to his name"* in front of a judge. His words not mine. Stupid, foolish, egocentric jerk.

"Seems not. I think he's been sliding more and more into some real mental health issues but the cops showing up on my behalf pushed him over. For years, he was this cool-as-a-popsicle abuser, but once the truth was revealed and his shiny exterior has been tarnished, he really took a nosedive."

"Your brow is all furrowed." He reached up with wet fingers to smooth my forehead. "Enough talk of that twat. This is our two-day holiday away from the rest of the world. I, for one, am looking forward to spending it doing nothing but lying about, making love, eating scones with clotted cream off your chest, and doing a bit of reading."

I wiggled about in the tub. "Do we even *have* scones and clotted cream? That's the first question that comes to my mind. The second is when can we break them out?"

"What do you think was in all those bloody bags from the market?"

"Clementine sparkling water?"

"Yes, okay, there were a few bottles of those, but there were also some tea purchases since your cupboards are woefully devoid of any quality tea bags."

I snickered at his vehemence when it came to tea. I loved him so much I'd even bought an electric kettle for him to use. You microwave one cup of water for your boyfriend once or use a generic tea bag from a box purchased at the dollar store, and—whoa, boy. That was a lesson learned.

Only Yorkshire Tea for Jameson Hennessy, if you please. The Brits are quite serious about their tea.

He continued. "And some of those biscuits you introduced me to."

"The Pepperidge Farm tea cookies."

"Yes, those." He wiggled about in excitement. "They're lovely with tea. I may have bought a few bags of those as well, to tide us over."

"Any cheesy puffs?" I hit him with my best sad puppy face.

"As if I would go shopping and not find you some cheesy doodly things." I slid close, hip to hip, and stole a fast kiss. Mm, he tasted of sweet clementine. "And scones with clotted cream. It's hell to find clotted cream in this barbaric country but there are a few stores that carry it."

"You love us Americans and you know it." I stole one more kiss, tossed back my sparkling water, and then stood. Jamie sat in the tub, staring up at me questioningly.

"Everything okay?" he asked.

"I am more than okay. I think it's time to break out the scones."

"Ah." He finished his fizzy orange drink, placed the glass on the edge of the redwood tub, and rose from the bubbles. The lights in the tub made his wet skin glisten. "Far be it for me to stand in the way of anyone having a scone."

We paused long enough to turn off the hot tub. I'd cover it and gather our glasses later. Right now, it was time to feed a rather hungry-looking Brit.

OUR FIRST DAY OF THE NOTHING-BUT-JAMIE-AND-CRAIG-Two-Day-Holiday started with me giving him a blowjob to help him wake up. It was payback for his amazing display of oral skills last night. His tongue could do glorious things with clotted cream. As could his fingers.

We spent an hour or so eating breakfast, then decided the day was too beautiful to be spent indoors reading and/or fucking. We'd work those activities in, obviously. We took a ride out to Newport Beach and chartered a whale-watching tour.

The catamaran was sleek and modern. We settled in, bouncing softly over bright blue waves, with some light snacks and wine coolers from the charter company. Jamie slathered sunscreen all over himself, citing his aversion to sun freckles on his soft English rose skin. We were about an hour from the port when a school of dolphins decided to swim alongside us, leaping up out of the sea and then diving back into rolling white caps.

We moved out a little farther into the Pacific. Jamie and I strolled around to the back of the three-sixty walkaround deck at the behest of the first mate, a strapping fellow with hair bleached nearly white from the sun and skin dark and supple as old shoe leather.

Off the port, we got our first view of a blue whale. Jamie ran to the railing, his LA Storm ballcap blowing off his head right as the mighty mammal breached, sending a large flock of seabirds to wing. The whale was mere yards from the right pontoon. It blew out a geyser of water that flew into the air thirty or so feet.

"Holy shit!" Jamie yelled, his glasses wet, as were our faces and hair.

The whale disappeared under the water, coming up on the other side of the boat. We ran to that side, phones out, and got to record it. Then a smaller whale appeared, the fluke slapping at the water dousing us yet again. Cells wet, hair sodden, clothes damp, we grinned at each other before exchanging a salty kiss. The two whales, a mother and calf, the first mate assumed, spent at least fifteen minutes swimming leisurely along with us until we lost them after they dove deep and disappeared.

"That was the most amazing thing I have ever seen," Jamie said on our way back to the harbor, a towel with the charter boat's logo on it around his neck. His cheeks were pink from the sun as his hat was now sitting on top of a tuna. "I love you so much for picking that excursion." The barking of seals and the raucous cries of gulls filled the air as we slowly made our way to the pontoon's berth. "Next stop is my pick."

"I'm all yours," I said, taking a moment before departing to sign a few hats for the crew of the whale-watching boat.

Jamie, being the scientist that he is, chose to spend the next few hours at the Griffith Observatory. We stopped at a Mexican eatery for a late lunch before driving up to our second destination. The famed observatory sat on a south-facing slope overlooking Los Angeles, Hollywood, and the Pacific Ocean. We walked through several exhibits, all dealing with space and the stars, hand-in-hand. Jamie was in his element. We then made our way to the Samual Oschin Planetarium where we saw two live shows. We spent some time outside on the roof, using the smaller telescopes to look at LA as dusk settled over the city. It was truly breathtaking. I could see why so many websites said this was a great date destination. My date was so excited over being able to discuss science with the tour guides that he offered me a choice as to how to end the day:

A – a queer nightclub for a cocktail.

B – a chance to ravage his arse.

I was not a dumb man. I chose B.

THE SECOND AND FINAL DAY OF OUR TWO-DAY WHIRLWIND of romance and fun times was spent making the drive out to Valyermo—which meant barren valley in Spanish, according to Jamie's mad skills in googling—to spend the day at a spa/ranch. This was totally my idea. Jamie had been less than thrilled when I sprang it on him over breakfast.

"Honestly, babe, when I said I wanted to spend the day riding a stud I didn't mean a damned horse. Do I look like the type who ever once played polo?"

His pout was cute but didn't sway me from the reservation I'd made late last night—after the ass-ravaging and when he was snoozing away contentedly. When he heard the word spa was part of the ranch's offering his frown turned upside down. Until we were in the stables at the ranch-slash-spa.

"Have I mentioned that I don't ride things bigger than

me?" Jamie pointed out as two pretty brown mares were being saddled for us.

"That's a fib," I whispered with a randy wink. He sniffed in that delightfully British way of his. "Come on, admit it, you think I look pretty good in tight jeans and a Stetson."

"I will concede that denim *does* look good on your bubble butt."

"Thank you. You'll enjoy it, I promise."

He didn't enjoy it. At all.

The mares—named Iris and Isis—were sisters and were the most docile beasts I had ever ridden. I'm not a master equestrian by any means, but I did like to get out into the sandy, rocky areas of California to ride when I could. Jamie was not a fan. He could ride, just barely, after an hour of basic instructions. We rode out with a guide named Paul who looked like Sam Elliott, right down to his silver mustache. Paul knew the trails well, as did the horses. After an hour, we stopped to have a light lunch alongside a narrow stream. There were some scrub trees to offer shade, and water for the horses. Paul made himself scarce after setting up our little meal on a redwood picnic bench.

When we lowered our backsides to the benches Jamie winced then threw me a glower over his dusty glasses.

"Let's make a point of not scheduling horseback riding after a double-header of arse-ravaging," he groaned while removing the cowboy hat he'd bought in the ranch's boutique. The fact that a dude ranch had a boutique said a lot about their clientele.

"Oh honey, I never even thought," I confessed then

reached over to take his hands in mine. "We can turn back."

"No, it's fine. It's a pleasant sort of pain," he whispered over a lunch of cold baked beans, soda biscuits, crispy fried bacon, and some canned fruit. Water was bottled. A real cowboy meal straight out of the saddle bags. "Reminds me of last night."

"Do you want me to ask Paul if he has a pillow?"

"Good God, no. He's too much a real cowpoke. Imagine the look he would give me. I wager he would call me a tenderfoot!"

"More like a tender ass," I teased softly and got a baking soda biscuit lobbed at my head.

With true British stoicism Jamie completed the ride back with a stiff upper lip. We hadn't dismounted properly, and he was off, with a rather awkward gait, to the spa area. I followed along at a snail's pace, checking my notifications now that we were back where there was some Wi-Fi. Nothing of any great import. A video from Claudia of her and Bruno visiting a dog park. Bruno wasn't too big on other dogs, but he adored children and was sitting beside a small girl who was attaching some of her bows to the long fur on his head and ears. He just sat there, soaking in the adoration and pretty decorations like a true diva.

I was so engrossed in the video, I nearly walked into the backside of a horse. Apologizing profusely to the rider and the horse, I hurried into the massive spa building. Soft tinkling bells and the smell of jasmine greeted me. As did a lean man with bright red hair in a gauzy white outfit. He handed me a drink in a tall glass.

"Hello and welcome to the revitalization center. My

name is Augustine Leo, and I'll be your guide through the luxury itinerary that you booked. Please enjoy the complimentary cocktails while we walk." I fell in behind him, walking past a small rock fountain and four people sitting on mats on the floor in front of the fountain, eyes closed, repeating some sort of mantra.

"First up we'll be joining your partner in the steam room. After your steam you'll have a cool shower then we'll be moving on to Thai herbal compress massages followed by fifteen minutes at the pool. After sun time, we'll move into a meditation suite where you'll have thirty minutes of silence and self-reflection with no cell phones or any outside interference."

He took a pause and smiled, and I thought he was done, but then he started up again.

Then we'll head back to the spa for a facial, a manicure, and a pedicure, and finally, you'll be free to join the other guests for dinner at the main ranch with more hearty Western fare. Or you can enjoy the sunset on the veranda of the spa, where you'll be served something from our healthy mind menu. The choice is yours."

"Okay."

"Mr. Hennessy is waiting for you in steam room six. This way, please."

I hurried to finish my cocktail, a fruity blend of pear, apple, lemon, and lime juices with a touch of vodka. It was really delicious. Augustine led me to a changing room where I stripped out of my horsey-smelling jeans and tee and into a red towel. My clothes would be laundered for me while I was being pampered.

Augustine then led me to one of several steam rooms. I

stepped in and gasped at the heat and moisture that slapped me in the face. Jamie was sprawled out over a bench, his glasses in a little pouch, his hair stuck to his head already.

I sat down beside Jamie, sweat flowing from me. It had to be well over a hundred and ten in here.

We proceeded to melt into puddles. When our time was up, we were given robes and then hustled to a shower room. The cool shower felt amazing, as did the dip in the pool, the massages, the mani/pedis, and the facial. The only thing I had some trouble with was not reaching for Jamie while sitting in a room with incense and Tibetan singing bowls vibrating harmoniously around me. All he had on was a spa robe cinched around his lean waist and nothing else. He'd refused to pull on his dirty briefs or the paper knickers, as he called them, so he was bare. I'd donned the disposable underwear and was kind of regretting it. They felt odd on my balls.

"I feel you looking at me in that way of yours," he said, sitting cross-legged on a mat with his eyes closed.

"I can't help looking at you that way. I love you. That's my dopey Craig-is-in-love look."

He cracked one eye open. "I love that look. Keep doing it."

And so, I did, through the meditation where I never meditated unless admiring your boyfriend was considered meditation. If so then I meditated the hell out of it.

During dinner on the verandah, as the sun set, I stared at him adoringly. My gaze never strayed from his beautiful profile as the sky changed colors from scarlet to blue and then to black. A hundred billion stars blinked to life, and I enjoyed the wonder on his face in the soft glow of small solar lights spaced about the large porch. Coyotes howled in the distance. An owl called out for a mate.

I'd never felt more at peace. Then my damn phone vibrated.

"Ugh," I sighed as I debated replying to the text or not. "Should have left on silent," I mumbled as I pulled it from my back pocket. The spa had treated us like royalty. Ten out of ten stars. Jamie had already said he wanted to return as soon as we could. Maybe we could live outside of the city someday, find a nearby place with a couple of houses, the girls could get horses, and I could finally have Bruno back. If I didn't lose him in court. And there he was. Fucking Leon.

"See who it is. If it's junk, then silence it," Jamie suggested before sipping his lemon/lime soda on the rocks. I read the text. Read it again. And then read it a third time. "You look odd. Is everything okay?"

"They found the delivery guy."

"What? Tell me."

"Get this. He's a client of Leon's and was trying to cross the border in a panic. It seems my ex made him an offer to dispose of evidence that would prove him guilty in an upcoming case if he did this one little favor for him. Then, when the deed was done, Leon told him to get the hell out of the country and never tell a soul, or he would ensure he died in prison."

"Bloody hell. That's got to be illegal?"

"According to Detective Russo, tampering with evidence is a huge no-no. Seems the guy is singing like Taylor Swift." I looked up from my phone. "I'm too scared to be excited."

He moved over to my lounge chair, hugged me tight, and then kissed me on the lips. Gently, with a smile that reached his pretty eyes.

"I give you permission to be as excited as you want to be."

So, I shot to my feet, taking him with me, and we danced a dance of pure joy under a desert moon.

Epilogue

Jamie

Returning home early from a seminar at the college, I wasn't expecting to find Oli and Jackson in such a focused huddle in our living room, especially not with Craig kneeling beside them, poring over what appeared to be a sprawl of blueprints and papers. The scene was domestic and intense, all at once.

Of course, I expected Oli and Jackson to be together every moment they could, given they'd come home from Disney an engaged couple, but to see Craig there as well made me smile. I couldn't be happier for my best friend, particularly when I knew I'd marry Craig one day.

I was sure of it.

Just as sure as two and two made four.

Talking of the man I'm going to marry. Craig's face lit up as he saw me, and he immediately beckoned me over with a wave and a grin that could brighten any room.

"Jamie, come take a look at this," he said, his excitement written in every line even before I reached them. "I can't make sense of the technical stuff, but look how gorgeous this is."

As I settled on the floor beside Craig, leaning in to view the plans more clearly, my eyes caught the detailed layout of a house. The drawings made it obvious that a lot of thought had gone into the design. Oli, who had always talked about buying a house, seemed to be making his dream a reality.

However, as I scanned the plans, a tinge of sadness brushed over me. There was no indication of an outbuilding or additional space that might suggest a place for me in their future setup. Not that I expected Oli and Jackson to plan their lives around me, but the realization stung a bit. They were a couple, and naturally, they would want their own space without an ever-present friend around. I guess I'd still see the girls; after all, I was part of their lives. Right?

"Post-retirement planning?" I asked as I placed the plans back on the table. He'd been talking about retiring for a couple of years, so it was a reasonable question.

Oli glanced at me, then reached for Jackson's hand and leaned into his lover. "It's time to think about what comes next."

Craig pushed the house specs back at me. "Look, though," he instructed, and I couldn't say no to his gorgeous smile or take my focus from his sapphire gaze. "Look," he instructed, so I did.

The plans showed a house with two studies, a large kitchen, and spacious living areas, but notably, it featured only two bedrooms. I frowned, puzzled, and poked at Oli's side.

"But what about the girls? They'll need their own rooms."

Oli looked up from a sheaf of papers, a smile playing on his lips as if he'd anticipated my confusion. "This isn't our house," he said, chuckling softly. "Our house is over here." He shifted the paperwork and pointed at the map. "This is us helping Craig look at potential designs for his house."

His house.

Yeah, I guess a man with a million-dollar career could afford to drop money on the house of his dreams.

"The next plot that is up against Oli's," Craig said, and he sounded so excited. "For us."

My confusion cleared instantly, replaced by a rush of surprise.

"For us?"

"Yep. We could build our own place, and the girls could just come over and visit all the time, and you wouldn't have far to go if you were caring for them and—"

"But you have a house."

He stared at me a moment, and then Oli dragged Jackson away as the silence went on. I hadn't meant to blurt that, but somehow all of his talking hadn't been making sense.

"This would be ours if you wanted it. I mean, I'm probably going to invest anyway, because it looks perfect, and I'm not like Oli, I won't wait to get traded away, I'll go first, so if you said yes to this then you'd have me for the long haul and Oli is staying here, and you'd be near Oli and the girls, and…"

"Craig?" I was lost for words.

"I'm not saying this right." He shifted quickly, straddling my lap, and cradling my face. "Build a house with me? Stay with me? Be with me? Forever?"

"A house," I said faintly, "I don't have the money to—"

"Babe," he stopped me and kissed me soundly. When he leaned away, I saw a hopeful glint in his eyes. He'd been considering the potential of starting something new, perhaps our own place together. "I love you. Do you love me?"

"Of course."

"There's no 'of course' about it."

"But there is," I defended. "I love you more than anything."

He bit his lip, then fake pouted. "More than math?"

I rolled my eyes. "It's maths."

"Tomatoes To-mar-tohs."

"It's maths because maths is short for—"

He stopped me with a kiss, and I willingly sunk into his embrace and held on tight. I could never get enough of the taste of him, or the weight of him in my lap. When we broke apart he was breathing heavily, and he was wild-eyed.

"I want forever with you," he blurted. "In our new house, next to Oli and the girls, will you build this with me? Live with me? Love me always?"

"Of course, I love you too."

Craig smiled at me. "Jamie, will you marry me?"

My heart skipped. "Sorry?"

"Marry me?" He leaned back so he could see my face.

"You're asking me to marry you?"

"I am. In our new backyard, on our land, where you've designed a maze full of spirals."

"I've always liked mazes," I said for something to say. "And spirals."

We kissed again, and this time we smiled and gripped each other tight.

"So will you?" he asked me again.

"Is the solution to the Riemann hypothesis still pending?" I deadpanned, and he blinked at me. Shit, why didn't I just say yes in a simple way?

"Huh?" he asked, confused.

"I mean, the solution to the Riemann hypothesis is still pending. So, it's a yes." He blinked more, and I realized I wasn't being clear at all. "That's me saying yes."

He kissed me then.

And it was a whole list of yesses in one touch.

It was an infinite amount of yesses.

It was forever.

THE END

Want to read about Oli & Jackson's wedding? Download your free copy of **Soulmate - rjscott.co.uk/soulmate**

With one groom in hiding and the backyard an explosion of pink, will this LA Storm wedding end in tears?

As his wedding day draws closer, Jackson is in the

throes of closing a high-stakes case working in conjunction with ATF and aimed at dismantling a notorious drug supply chain. The long hours and intense focus have left him exhausted and marginally grumpy. The wedding is now here, and all he has prepared for his vows is one line scribbled out on a crumpled, coffee-stained napkin. Then there's the shiner he got in a scuffle with an old silent movie star. Was there a witness protection program for guys who hosed up their big day?

With Scarlett and Daisy at the helm of wedding planning, Oli isn't surprised that the theme is a Barbie fantasy. As a compromise, the backyard venue is mostly a vision of understated elegance with pops of pink decorated with delicate spirals of lights that Jamie and the girls had spent hours hanging. However, as the wedding hour approaches and every detail falls perfectly into place, one crucial piece is missing—Jackson is hiding in the study and won't come out.

Hockey Series' from RJ Scott & V.L. Locey

Harrisburg Railers

Owatonna U Hockey

Arizona Raptors

Boston Rebels

LA Storm

Chesterford Coyotes - Young Adult

Harrisburg Railers

When hockey wunderkind Tennant Rowe meets his new coach, he knows he's in trouble. Jared Madsen is nine years older than Tennant, impossibly attractive, and — worst of all — his brother's off-limits best friend. Is their chemistry worth the risk?

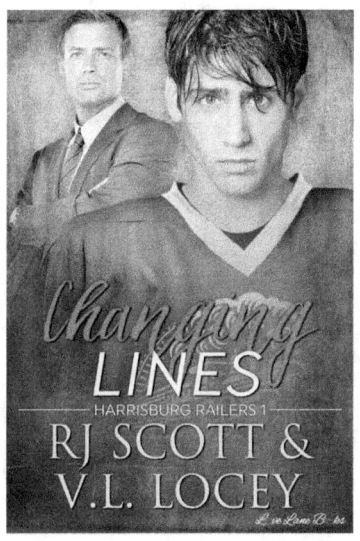

Changing Lines (Railers 1)

Can Tennant show Jared that age is just a number, and that love is all that matters?

The Rowe Brothers are famous hockey hotshots, but as the youngest of the trio, Tennant has always had to play against his brothers' reputations. To get out of their shadows, and against their advice, he accepts a trade to the Harrisburg Railers, where he runs into Jared Madsen. Mads is an old family friend and his brother's one-time teammate. Mads is Tennant's new coach. And Mads is the sexiest thing he's ever laid eyes on.

Jared Madsen's hockey career was cut short by a fault in his heart, but coaching keeps him close to the game. When Ten is traded to the team, his carefully organized world is thrown into chaos. Nine years his junior and his best friend's brother, he knows Ten is strictly off-limits, but as soon as he sees Ten's moves, on and off the ice, he knows that his heart could get him into trouble again.

Harrisburg Railers (Hockey Romance)

1. Changing Lines
2. First Season
3. Deep Edge
4. Poke Check
5. Last Defense
6. Goal Line
7. Neutral Zone
8. Hat Trick
9. Save The Date
10. Baby Makes Three
11. Rivals
12. Perfect Gifts
13. Family First

Railers Volume 1 | Railers Volume 2 | Railers Volume 3 | Railers Volume 4

Owatonna U, College Hockey

Meet the men of Owatonna University's hockey team

Ryker (Owatonna U, 1)

Ryker is hockey royalty, Jacob is a poor country boy. Can two vastly different people find common ground and become the men they want to be?

Ryker comes from a long line of championship-winning hockey players. Playing college hockey to develop his game is his only focus, and nothing will stand in the way of him working to become the best player. He has no room for relationships, people who point out his flaws, or anyone who calls him on his dreams. He certainly has no place for love, and meeting Jacob is nothing but a useful distraction on the side. After all trying to get his Owatonna Eagles teammate into bed is less work and more play. When tragedy rocks his family, his charmed life crumbles, and the only person he can turn to is the same one who claims to hate him.

Jacob Benson has only known hard work and stifling conservative values his whole life. Born and raised in the small rural community of Eden Crossing, Minnesota, he's the only son of a hard-working but struggling dairy farming family. Jacob is using his skills in hockey to finance his way to an agricultural science degree. These four years at Owatonna U. will probably be the only time he has to enjoy life, gain acceptance about his sexuality, and live openly before his inevitable return to the farm. Running into a pretty rich boy like Ryker Madsen is putting a damper on his enjoyment of life away from home. Ryker's flip, conceited, carefree attitude grates on Jacob's every nerve. So why, if Ryker is everything he dislikes, does he want nothing more than to explore the sinful dreams that his annoying teammate stars in every night?

Ryker

Owatonna U Hockey (Hockey Romance)

Arizona Raptors

Coast to Coast (Arizona Raptors 1)

Coast To Coast

**When opposites attract, this bottom-of-the-league team will
never be the same again.**

A stipulation in his father's will forces Mark back into the arms of
a family that disowned him and leaves him one-third owner of a
hockey team facing financial ruin. He doesn't even watch hockey,
let alone like it, and wants nothing more than to head back to
New York. Then there's the new coach, a stubborn, opinionated,
irritating man with superiority issues and questionable music

taste. Butting heads with Rowen becomes the new normal, but it comes with passionate debate and an all-consuming lust.

Challenged to rebuild one of the worst teams in the league into a future cup contender, Rowen can't pass up the opportunity. Never in his twenty years of hockey has he ever seen a team managed so badly or coached players overflowing with resentment and bigotry. Yet there's something about this team and this city that compels him to roll up his sleeves and start dismantling. If only Mark, one of three siblings who now own the Raptors, wasn't so damned rock-headed yet so damned appealing his job might be easier. It doesn't look like either is willing to give in, but one night in a dark, desert hotel changes everything.

Coast To Coast

Arizona Raptors (Hockey Romance)

1. Coast To Coast
2. Across the Pond
3. Shadow and Light
4. Sugar and Ice
5. School and Rock

Boston Rebels

Top Shelf (Boston Rebels 1)

Acting on the attraction to his best friend's brother has always been off the table for Xander until a passionate hookup with Mason at a beach resort begins a love affair that burns long after summer ends.

Mason specializes in assisting same-sex couples on their journey to becoming parents and fighting every rule that blocks his way in the stuck-in-the-past agency that hired him. Living in his brother's pool house is rent-free, and every cent he earns he saves for his dream—that one day he'd have his own company helping others. The downside is that he has to see his annoying brother every day, the upside is that his brother's teammates from the

Boston Rebels make regular visits. The eye candy that passes Mason's window is almost enough to make him consider dating a hockey player, but not just any player though. Ever since Xander —his brother's childhood friend—came out as gay at a press conference, Mason's puppy love has turned into a burning attraction he can no longer ignore.

Hockey has been one of Xander's main focuses since he was old enough to balance on skates. Well, hockey and Mason Kingsley, but Mason was always unattainable. Now that he's about to see thirty candles on his birthday cake and is no longer hiding the fact he's gay, he's ready to find a soul mate to make his life complete. A summer vacation is just what he needs to have time to think, but when the Boston Rebels arriving in paradise with Mason in tow, thinking is the last thing he needs. One torrid night under a balmy moon and rules about not messing with his best friend's brother vanish on a warm, tropical breeze.

Summer romances don't generally last past Labor Day, but with the new season about to begin Xander and Mason are going to have to face the world and decide if their love is real enough to withstand everything.

Boston Rebels

Lost In Boston (Free Prequel Novella)

1. Top Shelf
2. Back Check
3. Snowed
4. Royal Lines
5. Blade
6. Rental

LA Storm

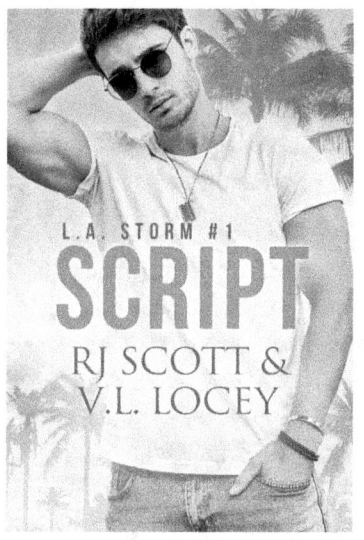

Script (LA Storm, 1)

Script

Hollywood A-lister Finn might be Canadian, but he needs Cameron to show him how to hockey.

Actor Finn Kerrigan is at a crossroads. After growing up a soap star, then starring in a hugely successful trilogy of action movies, he's finally given the chance to read a heartfelt and passionate script that could change his life forever. The role would be enough for people to see him as a serious actor, and maybe even win him an award or two (and no, a golden raspberry award for his action movies doesn't count). Once established as a serious actor he's sure he can come out of the closet and finally live his truth. When he lies to get the part of a hockey player on a struggling team, he suddenly has nowhere to hide. He might be Canadian, but the last time he skated he was ten, and no, he doesn't have hockey in his blood. With only a month until filming starts, he about to be exposed, but partnered with a player who's supposed to be giving him tips, he doesn't realize how many of his secrets will come to light. Falling in lust, one heated kiss at a time, is inevitable, but giving Cameron up at the end of the shoot could break his heart.

Cameron Chavkin is the face of the LA Storm. And the body, and the hair, and the smile. He's at the prime of his career, men and women want to be with him, and he's skating better than he ever has before. His house sits next to a famous rock star's mansion, his garage is filled with expensive cars, and he's even been asked to mentor a once-famous actor in a new hockey movie. Life is pretty sweet. Until the bad boy of hockey meets Finn, a man on the edge with more secrets than Cameron has endorsements. Knowing better than to get involved, Cameron is swept up despite himself, and when it's time to say goodbye to the Storm's most eligible bachelor is finding it hard to follow the script.

Script

LA Storm

Chesterford Coyotes, Young Adult Romance

Off The Ice (Chesterford Coyotes, 1)

Off The Ice

A coming-of-age love story with high school, hockey rivalry, friendship, family, and coming out.

Soren's life changes in an instant when he and his younger brother are adopted by hockey royalty. Making sense of his new life is hard enough, but when he's enrolled in a private school it means facing a whole new set of problems. Navigating friendship, family, and hockey is one thing, but being attracted to the boy who vexes him is a whole new thing.

Felix has a reputation to protect. He's the kid who seems to have everything but looks can be deceiving. Spinning lies about his perfect life, he's created a fantasy world that even he has started to believe. Only, it's not long before everything crumbles, all of his pretty lies are revealed, and only his closest rival sees through his pain and stands by him.

Fighting is easy, friendship is hard, but love is everything.

Off The Ice

Chesterford Coyotes

1. Off The Ice
2. On Thin Ice
3. *Dance on Ice*

Also By RJ Scott

For a full list of ebooks and links please scan the code above or
visit rjscott.co.uk/rjbooks

Meet RJ Scott

RJ discovered romance in books at a very young age and realized that if there wasn't romance on the page, she could create it in her head. With over one hundred and fifty books published, she is a full time author of gay romance.

She lives and works out of her home in the beautiful English countryside, spends her spare time reading, watching films, and enjoying time with her family.

The last time she had a week's break from writing she didn't like it one little bit and has yet to meet a box of chocolates she couldn't defeat.

www.rjscott.co.uk | rj@rjscott.co.uk

NEWSLETTER - rjscott.co.uk/rjnews

facebook.com/author.rjscott

x.com/Rjscott_author

instagram.com/rjscott_author

amazon.com/author/rj-scott

bookbub.com/authors/rj-scott

goodreads.com/rjscott

pinterest.com/rjscottauthor

Also By VL Locey

For a full list of ebooks and links please scan the code above or
visit vllocey.com/stories-from-vl-locey

Meet V.L. Locey

V.L. Locey loves worn jeans, yoga, belly laughs, walking, reading and writing lusty tales, Greek mythology, the New York Rangers, comic books, and coffee.

(Not necessarily in that order.)

She shares her life with her husband, her daughter, one dog, two cats, a flock of assorted domestic fowl, and two Jersey steers.

When not writing spicy romances, she enjoys spending her day with her menagerie in the rolling hills of Pennsylvania with a cup of fresh java in hand.

vllocey.com
vicki@vllocey.com

Newsletter - vllocey.com/newsletter

facebook.com/V.L.Locey

x.com/vllocey

instagram.com/vl_locey

bookbub.com/authors/v-l-locey

goodreads.com/vllocey

pinterest.com/vllocey